Nick's Blues

Nick's Blues

John Harvey

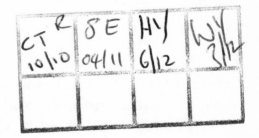

W F HOWES LTD

This large print edition published in 2009 by
W F Howes Ltd
Unit 4, Rearsby Business Park, Gaddesby Lane,
Rearsby, Leicester LE7 4YH

1 3 5 7 9 10 8 6 4 2

First published in the United Kingdom in 2008
by Five Leaves Publications

A CIP catalogue record for this book is available
from the British Library

ISBN 978 1 40743 355 4

Typeset by Palimpsest Book Production Limited,
Grangemouth, Stirlingshire
Printed and bound in Great Britain
by MPG Books Ltd, Bodmin, Cornwall

FSC
Mixed Sources
Product group from well-managed
forests and other controlled sources
Cert no. SGS-COC-2953
www.fsc.org
© 1996 Forest Stewardship Council

CHAPTER 1

Four days after Nick Harman's seventh birthday, his father climbed onto a bridge high above four lanes of traffic, paused, then threw himself to his death on the road below. That was a little over nine years ago. Today Nick was sixteen.

The clock alongside the bed read 7:59.

Nick reached out an arm and switched off the alarm before it could ring. When he'd been small, little more than three or four, not yet started school, his dad had sneaked into his room while he was asleep and fixed stars in the shapes of constellations to the ceiling above his bed. The kind that shone in the dark.

Nick lay there now and stared upwards, trying to make out the faintest glow.

Not so much later he realised that his eyes had closed again. 8:07. He could have risked a few minutes more but he needed to pee. The quilt had become tangled around his legs and he tugged it free and swung his feet round towards the floor. He could hear music, blurred, from the flat upstairs; sounds of traffic, impatient, from the street.

Wearing the t-shirt and boxer shorts in which he'd slept, Nick headed for the bathroom.

Fifteen minutes later, dressed, dark hair still tangled, he pushed open the kitchen door. The radio was playing, tuned to Capital, and he switched it to Radio One then XFM then off. Chris had lent him the new Radiohead album and would be on to him to find out what he thought. The water in the kettle was still warm and, setting it to boil, he reached down a mug and dropped a tea bag ready inside. If his mum had not already left for work, he might have had toast instead of corn flakes. Before she got this new job, seven to four six days a week behind one of the tills at the petrol station shop, that's what she'd made, most mornings, toast and jam, toast and marmalade. Time to nag him about being late, his homework, the state of his shoes.

The envelope was propped up against the box of cereal, not quite stuck down. A ten pound note folded inside the card. *Happy Birthday, Love Mum.* Nick stirred two sugars into his tea and glanced at the clock.

His rucksack was heavy as usual, weighted down with books, and he swung it on to one shoulder as he pulled the door fast shut and turned the key. The one time he'd forgotten to lock it, some opportunistic shit off the estate had been in there and out again before Nick, half-way to school, had realised his mistake and come running back. The forty quid that his mum kept

2

for emergencies had gone, a watch, bits and pieces of jewellery she scarcely ever wore, the computer from Nick's room that wasn't yet paid for, the video and the TV. These last two had been replaced, but the only times Nick got to go on a computer were at school or round his mates' evenings or weekends.

From the forecourt outside the flats a narrow path led down towards the street. A car body shop to one side and on the other a patch of grass dedicated to the memory of some councillor who, if he saw the state of it, food wrappings and drying dog turds, would be turning in his grave. There had been some small flowers growing there a month or so before, white and purple, but now they had died away.

Faintly, Nick could see his breath on the air.

There were two comprehensives in the area, close together, one bog standard, the other Roman Catholic, and the road Nick walked along now was crowded on both sides with clusters of three or more pupils, talking, smoking, pushing, shouting, carelessly forcing anyone else off the pavement as they passed. The younger ones wore a semblance of uniform, the rest dressed in some combination of combats or track pants, t-shirts and hoodies, some with logos, some not; trainers by Nike or Adidas, occasionally Puma or New Balance. A scattering of girls wore calf-length coats in black or beige, short skirts over coloured tights; wide-fitting jeans hung low on the hips of some of the boys, hoods pulled forward over their heads. Nike again. Tommy Hilfiger. Gap.

Nick, in red tab Levi's and a faded denim jacket, his boots knock-off Timberlands from a stall on Camden Market, hurried on, snatches of conversation drifting around him.

'. . . that's shit, man, why d'you watch that shit?'

'Offside? Course he wasn't bloody offside!'

'. . . in the queue outside the Boston, wasn't he, just standing there, right, not saying nothin' and this bloke bottled him.'

'Fit, i'n it? Really fit.'

'Look at that, I wouldn't mind a bit of that.'

'Forget it, she's a slag.'

Nick saw his mates Christopher and Scott standing outside the school entrance, Christopher's head moving slightly to whatever was playing on his Walkman, Scott sharing a smoke with his girl friend, Laura.

Christopher was tall, almost six foot, only just beginning to thicken out; most days he dressed like he was about to go off and climb a mountain somewhere, anorak, waterproof trousers with a million pockets, walking boots with serious cleats. Scott was shorter, smarter, almost always in some variation of black and grey, laughing now at something Laura had just said.

Laura had a sharp face and blonde spiky hair and went to the Catholic school across the road. She and Scott had been going out the best part of a year – some kind of a record.

'You listen to the Radiohead yet?' Christopher asked.

Nick shook his head.

Laura's face brightened with a grin. 'I saw Ellen just now,' she said.

When, a month or so back, Nick had asked who was the girl with the yellow waterproof and the black beret, Laura had walked right over and asked her if she fancied going out with one of her boy friend's mates.

'Sorry,' the message had come back, 'she says you're not her type.'

And they'd laughed at the embarrassment colouring Nick's face.

A few days later he'd learned her name.

'Come on,' Christopher said, removing his headphones. 'Else we'll be bollocked for being late.'

Nick nodded, hands stuffed down into his pockets against the cold.

Laura turned away and waited for the traffic to stop at the crossing and the three boys walked together into school.

CHAPTER 2

The block of flats, five storeys high, where Nick and his mother lived, had been built in 1936. Whenever Nick read the inscription embedded into the wall of yellowing brick, he wondered it had stood that long.

By the time Nick's parents had moved in, roughly fourteen years ago, the estate had spread like a kid's game of Lego, long and narrow, tall and thin, none of the parts quite matching. Concrete and glass. The entrances to each block now had doors that locked, numbers that you punched in to gain admission. One look at the squares of garden or up at the balconies was enough to tell you who had been living there half a lifetime, who had been moved in by the council as a last resort. If anywhere stayed empty for too long it was squatted in or worse.

Most days after school, Nick hung out with Christopher and Scott, having a Coke or some chips at the same café where they bought a slice of pizza for lunch. In the summer they'd go and sit on the grass in the open space which bordered the main road, sometimes kicking a ball about or just lazing round and looking at the girls. Talking about who they'd like to have if they got the chance.

More often than not, Nick would end up walking Christopher back to where he lived, a tall Victorian house on one of the tree-lined streets beyond the estate, Saabs and SUVs parked along the kerb.

On the way they'd chat about this and that, arguing over the respective merits of Arsenal and Chelsea, Eduardo or Ballack; Nick listening to Christopher as he rubbished some singer for her lyrics or the way she kept veering out of tune. Not that Nick cared one way or another. There was a poster of J-Lo on his wall and it wasn't there because he liked the way she sang.

Sometimes when they got to Christopher's they'd go up to his room and mess around on the computer, but this was one of the evenings when Nick worked so he headed back quite soon, following a ramshackle series of walkways through the estate.

'Hey, Nick! Nicky, where you goin'?'

'Yeah, man, what's your hurry?'

Hands in the pockets of his jacket, Nick continued walking, not breaking his stride. He could see Ross Blevitt and his mates standing round in the shadow of the tower block, hoods pulled up, the sound of Dr Dre or Ice T distorting from the open windows of the ground floor corner flat. Blevitt with his Burberry cap pulled well forward on his head and a surly smile on his seventeen year old face.

'Hey, Nicky. Chill.'

'He can't,' called someone else. 'Hurry home to his mama, i'n it?'

'Yeah, Nicky. Give her one for me.'

Recognising the voice, Nick half-turned into the laughter and saw Blevitt, cap pushed back now, leering as he cupped his crotch with one hand.

Blevitt had started on him once, a year or so back, and Nick had stood his ground, the pair of them pretty evenly matched and neither willing to strike the first blow. Nick knew that Blevitt felt he had lost face and had been looking for a way of getting back at him ever since.

'He's a pussy,' someone shouted.

'Mama's pussy.'

Slowly, Blevitt moved his hand up from his crotch, fingers extended then curling, beckoning him on. His crew behind him, seven or eight strong.

This wasn't the time.

Not hurrying, deliberate, Nick resumed walking, jeers and catcalls falling about his shoulders as he continued on his way.

'Nicky, is that you?'

Nick suppressed his usual 'Who d'you think?' and carried on into his room, draped his jacket across the back of the chair and dumped his rucksack on the narrow bed.

'Nicky?'

His mum was sitting at the table in the small

kitchen, leafing through one of her magazines. In the living room the television was playing to no one, volume low.

'There's tea in the pot.'

''S'okay.'

Opening the fridge door, he fished out a can of Lucozade.

'That stuff'll rot your teeth.'

'Like yours, you mean?'

His mother sighed and turned the page.

Nick took two slices of bread from their wrapping, rummaged some more in the fridge, then spread the bread with peanut butter and black-currant jam before pressing the pieces together. Forestalling his mother's complaint, he put the sandwich on a plate and sat opposite her, chair rocked back on its rear legs.

'How was school?'

He shot her a look and she caught herself wondering when the ritual response of 'Fine' had been replaced by that familiar expression of boredom and disdain.

'There's oven chips in the freezer. I could do you egg and chips.'

'It's okay, I'll get something at work.'

'Suit yourself.'

Three evenings a week and alternate weekends, Nick had a job in the restaurant attached to one of the local pubs. For £4.50 an hour, cash in hand, he would clear the tables and wipe them down, load the dishwasher, dry plates and scrub pans; at the end of a session he would clean out the gunge and grease that had collected in the sump of the main sink, scald the chopping surfaces with boiling water, spray and polish the griddle till it shone.

Working two jobs, the petrol station and some evenings behind the bar, his mum earned enough to put food on the table and pay the rent, keep Nick in basic clothes. Anything extra he had to earn for himself. And he had his heart set on a scooter, a Vespa or maybe even a Piaggio. For every pound he spent, there were three or four he saved.

'What time you leaving?'

Nick looked at the clock. 'Soon.'

'Hang on then. There's something for you.'

When she came back into the room, she kissed him on the cheek. 'Happy birthday.' The package in her hand was the size of a shoe box and at first Nick thought it was the trainers he'd been after, but when he picked it up the weight wasn't right and besides whatever was inside rattled.

'What is it?'

'Open it. Look for yourself.'

'What is it?' he repeated.

'I don't know.'

Nick narrowed his eyes. The box was wrapped in brown paper, a section of which had faded as though it had been left somewhere in the sun. Along the edges, the paper had been fastened down with Sellotape and for good measure the whole thing was tied around with string.

'Your dad left it for you. With a note. He wanted you to have it on your birthday. When you were sixteen.' She wasn't looking at him as she spoke.

'What note? What bloody note?'

'I burned it, threw it away, I can't remember.'

'You must remember.'

'All right. I burned it. That and everything else he left.'

The inside of Nick's chest felt hollow.

'Everything except that.'

Though there was no more than a mouthful of tea left in her cup and that was cold, she brought it to her lips.

Nick stared at the box: the way it rested on the table between them.

'I'm gonna be late for work,' Nick said, pushing back his chair. 'I've got to change.'

His mother took her cup to the sink and rinsed it, went into the living room and turned up the sound on the TV. A few minutes later, she heard the front door open and then close.

CHAPTER 3

Next morning Nick was late. Hurrying between the last stragglers, his rucksack bounced awkwardly against his back, first drops of rain fresh on his face. His mates had given him up and gone inside.

Christopher he caught up with on the way to maths mid-morning, the first class they shared.

'You okay?' Christopher asked.

'Yeah, why?'

'Thought you'd decided to bunk off.'

'Then I wouldn't be here now, would I?'

Christopher decided to keep the rest of his questions to himself.

'What happened to you this morning?' Scott asked later. They were on their way, the three of them, to the café for their usual slice. The rain had eased off, but overhead the sky was still grey.

'What d'you mean, what happened?' Nick said. 'Nothing happened. I was a few minutes late, that's all.'

'You're never late.'

'Yeah? Well, today I was, okay?'

Scott shrugged and spat at the ground.

Nick said nothing.

Outside the café Laura was waiting for them, takeout cappuccino in her hand – that and a couple of Marlborough Lights were all she normally had for lunch. Maybe a bite of Scott's pizza.

'I thought you weren't here,' she said, looking up at Nick.

'Jesus,' Nick said.

'Leave him,' Christopher said.

'Laying in bed thinking about Ellen,' Laura said with a grin. 'Stunt your growth.'

'You can talk,' Scott said.

'That's cause I'm thinking about you.'

'You better be.'

'We gonna eat or what?' Nick said, and suddenly there she was, Ellen, right across the street. Walking with four or five other girls, not wearing her beret today, her streaked fair hair partly masking her face until, with a laugh, she shook it free.

Laura had followed the direction of Nick's gaze and was about to make another crack but something in his expression made her bite her tongue.

'What you having?' Christopher asked, digging Nick in the ribs. 'Ham and cheese?'

'Yeah,' Nick said. 'Why not?'

It was the cheapest they did.

Nick had been awake that morning since well before six, waking out of a dream that splintered the moment he rolled onto his side to look at the clock. Sweat matted his hair to his scalp. The water

13

in a glass by the bed tasted stale. In the restaurant the night before, a party of eight had insisted on sitting around till way past twelve, ordering brandy after brandy and laughing at their own jokes. Eventually, Marcus, the manager, had tapped Nick on the shoulder.

'Cinderella, go home.'

'Nah, it's okay,' Nick had said. 'I'll stay.'

'I can't afford overtime, I've told you before.'

'It doesn't matter.'

Marcus had thrown Nick's jacket at him by way of reply.

There had been no more than the usual selection of drunks on the street. Only the usual deals going down outside the all-night garage and the twenty-four hour corner store.

He could hear the faint wheeze of his mother's breathing as soon as he got inside, the door to her room ajar. Two years ago now, she'd cut down her smoking to five a day; this after a friend, early forties like herself, had just survived a cancer scare.

Nick had been on to her to quit altogether since a health education lecture they'd had at school, the pictures of smokers' lungs, shrivelled and blackened as burned-out shells. A lot of the other kids had been laughing as they left the hall, couldn't wait to light up as soon as they hit the street, but Nick believed what he saw, knew that it was real.

People dying.

The box was still where it had been left, at the centre of the kitchen table.

How long did it take to die?

Months, seconds, years?

Growing up, he had walked, some empty Saturday or Sunday afternoons, along the Archway Road until he was almost underneath the bridge and stood there staring up, and sometimes he would see a small wedge of colour amongst the bridge's grey, the face of someone peering down.

Sometimes he had tried to imagine his father's fall.

What had been in his mind.

Lifting the box, Nick held it to his ear and, much as he had believed, when younger, that if you held a sea shell to your ear you could hear the sea, what he heard now was the wind rushing past his father's body as he fell.

Nick dropped the box as if his fingers burned.

Awake early, he lay in bed, listening to his mother getting ready to leave, the bedroom door, the bathroom, kettle, radio, the bathroom door again, a few snatches of song. When she had gone, he hurried to the kitchen and brought the box back to his room.

The knots on the string were tight and small and it was all Nick could do to work first one corner and then another free; one tug at the tape and it peeled loose in a single strip. He began by folding the brown paper back then screwed it, impatiently, into a ball. He started counting beneath his breath and on five the lid lifted easily free.

The contents were loosely held inside a newspaper dated 1994.

Nick's first thought was that his father had tipped the contents of a drawer into the box with little reason. Scraps of paper, photographs, torn tickets, an audio cassette, guitar picks, what he thought was a capo, several spare guitar strings, a mouth organ in a torn green plastic case.

Nick's eyes went to the photographs first, shuffling them quickly through his fingers: his father on stage with other musicians or alone; smiling at the camera in what seemed to be a restaurant; a woman walking by the sea. His father again, out of doors somewhere, grass and trees, and in his arms – on one arm to be exact – a baby resting against his chest, eyes open, staring up. The look on his father's face as he gazed back down.

Seeing it, Nick's breath caught and a sob broke from his throat.

He wasn't going to let the bastard make him cry.

As Nick lay back down and pulled the covers over his head, the contents of the box scattered everywhere.

Instead of going to Christopher's after school that day, he went straight home. Not long in, still wearing her petrol station overall, his mother was talking to someone on the phone. Nick grunted and hurried to his room. Seeing the Hoover out in the hall, he thought she might have reneged on their deal, gone in and tidied up, moved things around, but no, everything was where he had left it, strewn across the bed, the floor.

Sitting, he tried the guitar picks on his fingers, fingers and thumb, the plastic hard against his skin; his dad must have had small hands, not small necessarily but long and thin. He looked at them in one of the photographs, his father seated on a stool playing, concentration tightening his face. The fingers of the left hand were pressed high against the strings, the others curled over the centre of the instrument in a blur, too fast for the camera to clearly catch.

His father's face was lean, his eyes were dark; in some pictures he was clean shaven, in others he had a beard, a small goatee. Carefully, Nick spread the photographs along the bed – six, seven, eight – searching them for some resemblance to himself.

'Nick? You all right in there?' His mother's voice from behind the door.

'Yeah, fine.'

'Want some tea? I've made some tea.'

'Okay.'

Only then did he realise that the young woman his father was sitting with in one of the photos was his mother. Taken later than the others it must have been, his father older, his arm around her shoulders, her face turned to him while he looked out at the camera and smiled.

17

Cheese!

She was pretty then, his mum. Nick could see that, her hair pulled back into a pony tail. And young. Not so much older than the girls he sat with every day at school. How old could she have been? He had no idea. Nineteen? Twenty? Twenty-one?

Holding the photograph closer, he studied her expression and saw happiness, uncertainty.

'Nicky, this tea's getting stewed.'

'I'm coming, all right?'

Sliding the photographs together, he placed them carefully at the bottom of the box.

As well as the tea, there was a sponge cake on the table, jam and cream, icing sugar dusted across the top.

'No candles, I'm afraid.'

'And it's a day late.'

'Well, d'you want some or not?'

'Yeah, might as well.'

Nick was on his second piece before he felt able to ask.

'Why d'you want to know that?' his mother said, amused.

Nick shrugged.

'You've never asked before.'

'I'm asking now.'

'Is this something to do with whatever was in that box?'

'Just tell me.'

'Twenty. I was twenty, all right. Satisfied?'

'And my dad, how old was he?'

'When I met him? I don't know. Forty-three, forty-four.'

'What?'

'He was old enough to be your father.'

'Well, he wasn't, was he? He was yours.'

From the pocket of her uniform, she took a packet of cigarettes.

'I thought you were giving up,' Nick said.

'I'll do what I want.'

'Yeah, right.'

'What's that mean?'

'Nothing.'

They stared at one another across the table, until his mother reached for her lighter and Nick pushed away his plate and cup and headed for the door.

'Nick. Nicky, don't. Come back.'

When the front door slammed, she sat back down with a sigh and drew the smoke from the cigarette down deep into her lungs.

CHAPTER 4

Nick walked without really thinking where he was going. Down on to the main road and left instead of right: the opposite direction to school. In less than five minutes he'd drawn level with the place where he worked and hurried past, not wanting to be recognised. Then the church that had been taken over by hippies and crusties until the police moved them on; holy rollers in there now, Baptists or whatever, Nick had heard them clapping and singing Sunday mornings, the men in suits and ties, little girls in pink dresses, their hair in pigtails or braids.

He stopped to look at the posters outside the old cinema that was now a music venue. The Cult. Apocalyptica. The Long Blondes. Along with Christopher and Scott, he'd tried to blag his way into the club night a few times, Saturdays late, the queue stretching down the street. Once they'd succeeded in making it past the bouncers, twice been turned away. He remembered the music loud inside, the crack of plastic glasses being trodden underfoot, the smell of cannabis everywhere. Two blokes with folded arms blocking the entrance to the Gents: 'You don't want to go in there.' Someone tapping him on the shoulder at the bar, trying to sell him a tab of E. Then this girl, half-pissed or more, launching herself at Scott with a giggle and pushing her tongue right down his throat.

'You could've had her,' Christopher said later, heading for the exit.

'So could anyone.'

They should try and go again, Nick thought.

He felt warm and it wasn't simply that he'd been walking fast. In the Bull and Gate he ordered a pint of lager and when the barman challenged him for ID he tried to brazen it out and lost. Further along, he went into McDonald's and bought a cheeseburger and fries and sat near the window staring out.

Why had he lost his temper? What had all that been about?

His mum had married some bloke her own age, he'd still be around today? Who was he kidding? More than half the kids he knew at school were living with one parent instead of two. Scott got to see his old man three times a year if he was lucky. Christopher's mum had moved out a few years back and now his dad was shacked up with some Bulgarian slapper who used to be Chris's baby sitter.

He thought about his mother's expression in the photograph: she'd been happy, hadn't she?

He remembered when he'd been nine or ten and

had a thing about McDonald's apple pies his mum would buy him one, a treat, Saturdays when they were out doing the shopping. He remembered how the apple, once he'd bitten through the brittle crust, had always been too hot and burned his tongue.

Finished, Nick emptied his trash into the bin and pushed back outside. The drum set in the music shop window sparkled in the overhead light alongside a line of red and gold electric guitars, nothing old and acoustic like the one his dad had played.

'Let's form a band,' Scott had said one afternoon. They were upstairs in Christopher's house, passing round a spliff and listening to White Stripes.

'All right,' Nick had said. 'Who's gonna play what?'

'Who cares?'

Aside from Christopher, who had grade three piano, none of them could play a thing. Or sing.

It didn't stop them spending the next hour thinking up names: Omerta (Christopher had been watching documentaries on BBC Four again), The Missing, Moving Targets, Casey and the Unknowns.

'Who's Casey?' Nick had asked.

'Nobody knows.'

Which had been enough to have them falling about laughing, eventually recovering enough to go downstairs and raid the kitchen for some munchies, a packet of chocolate chip cookies, half a Mr Kipling fruit pie, the remnants of some blackberry and apple crumble from the back of the fridge.

Nick looked at his watch. It was starting to get dark. He had three lots of homework and the deal he'd made with himself about studying on those nights he wasn't working seemed in danger of being forgotten. Heading back, he took a short cut between the backs of the houses, a narrow alley that passed eventually beneath the railway bridge, emerging close to where he lived.

Midway along he heard someone running fast in his direction and two youths burst past, forcing him to flatten himself against the crumbling wall or be sent flying. He couldn't be sure, both were wearing sports tops with the hoods pulled well over their heads, but one of them Nick thought he might have recognised.

Minutes later, skirting an abandoned refrigerator which had been pulled down on to its side, he heard the siren of a police car drawing closer and then fading. If his mum was still in when he got back he'd apologise for going off at half-cock. There were questions he wanted to ask and if she was in a mood she'd never tell him anything.

He slowed down passing under the bridge, darker there and God knows what he might step in. Twenty metres further along the alley opened out on to the road and he was almost home. As his feet touched the pavement, a police car, travelling fast, swung hard across and came to a squealing halt in front of him, blocking his path.

Nick's instinct was to run.

Car doors were thrown open and two uniformed officers jumped out.

'Okay, son. Take it easy. We just want a word.'

The one who spoke was big, with ginger hair, six two or three, the other one younger, smaller, pimples livid on his face.

'Where you off to?' Ginger said.

'Home.'

'Where's that?'

Nick told him.

'What's your name?'

Nick told him that too.

'Watch him,' Ginger said, moving back towards the car. The other officer nodded and took a step closer, while Ginger repeated Nick's name into the handset clipped to his uniform.

'What's this about?' Nick asked.

No reply.

Gawking, a couple on the opposite side of the street walked slowly past.

'Okay, son,' Ginger said, stepping back. 'Why don't you just get in the car?'

'What?'

'Get in the car.'

'What for?'

'Just a few questions, at the station.'

'What questions?'

'At the station.'

There was a woman with two shopping bags now, on her way from the bus stop, standing there staring.

'Come on,' Ginger said, not unkindly. 'We haven't got all night.'

Nick didn't know what else to do. He ducked his head beneath the officer's hand and the rear door was closed firmly behind him. Moments later they were pulling away.

CHAPTER 5

Dawn Harman hadn't been able to get him out of her mind: Les, her former husband, Nick's father. Not since handing over the box the previous morning. The box she'd come so close to throwing away a hundred times. And then, that evening, when Nick had started asking those questions about when she and Les had first met . . .

It had been a pub over by Highbury Corner, a room upstairs, some kind of – what was it? – acoustic evening. Not the kind of thing Dawn went in for at all, not then anyway, but one of her friends had said it might be a laugh, said she'd been before.

Well, it wasn't a laugh at all, not exactly.

The room was cold and draughty, no heating. Benches and tables, candles, a handful of rickety chairs. She'd kept her coat on most of the evening, only taking it off to fold it across her legs in at attempt to keep them warm. Slide her hands down underneath. And the acts, most of them, had been dire: a couple of singers mumbling, lovelorn, over their guitars; a man with carroty hair who ranted on about striking miners, a hand clapped the whole time over one ear; a poet with dreadlocks; this Irish bloke playing the penny whistle and jigging around in hob-nail boots. And then there'd been Les.

She hadn't noticed him before, no reason to, just one of those blokes hanging round the bar. Not till he stepped out front to a smattering of applause. Leather trousers, boots with a heel, waistcoat unbuttoned over a denim shirt; his hair was long, longer than she liked, his beard trimmed and dark.

The thing that struck her first, he seemed more professional than the rest. He had had his own equipment for one thing, amplifier and microphone. And the way he spoke, straight out at the audience, direct, no mumbling. Confident.

'Hi, I'm Les Harman.'

Even in the murk of that room, you could see the blue of his eyes.

'What d'you think?' her friend said. 'Nice looking, isn't he?'

Dawn thought she could never fancy a bloke who wore denim shirts, it just wasn't her style.

Quietly, Les ran his thumb over the strings of his guitar, made some small adjustment to the microphone and, satisfied, hooked one of his heels over the rung of the stool.

'I'd like to start off with an old Big Bill Broonzy song, especially for any of you heading back down to Balham or Clapham Junction via the Angel. It's "Southbound Train".'

Dawn didn't remember the rest in detail, one tune fading into another, her friend leaning forward, never taking her eyes off him, and Les acknowledging the applause for each song with a slightly self-conscious laugh before sliding into the next.

'The good news,' Les announced, 'I've got just one more before the interval. The bad, I'll be back later.'

After chatting to a couple of obvious fans, he came over to where they were sitting. 'I was wondering,' he said, 'if I could buy you ladies a drink?'

Dawn's friend blushed and mumbled agreement; Dawn's 'No, thank you,' was firm and clear.

'Some other time perhaps,' Les said and held her gaze.

On the way out she slipped one of the fliers advertising his future gigs into her pocket.

After that – she didn't want to think about after that.

Now she looked round at the clock, wondering how long it would be before Nick calmed down and came back home. Most likely he'd gone round to his mate Christopher's, taking it out on some video game.

She was leafing through the paper, looking to see what was on the television, when the phone rang.

That'll be him now, she thought, crossing to pick it up.

'Hello,' the voice said. 'Is that Mrs Harman?'

'Who's this?' Someone wanting me to change my gas supplier, she thought, those people never give up.

'This is Holmes Road Police Station. We have your son, Nick, here . . .'

'Nick? What's happened? Is he all right?'

'If you could come down to the station, Mrs Harman . . .'

'What's this all about? Is he in trouble?'

'If you could come down . . .'

'Nick, have you arrested him or something? What's he done?'

'As of now, Mrs Harman, we just want to ask him some questions. If it's not convenient for you to come yourself, we can always contact a social worker . . .'

'You'll do no such bloody thing. I'll be there as soon as I can.'

If she rang for a cab it would likely be fifteen, twenty minutes before one arrived and she could walk it in less; as it was, a C2 was coming along when she reached the main road and she jumped on that. Nick had been taken into the station and then left sitting in a corner while the two officers who'd brought him in conferred with the sergeant behind the desk. There were glances in his direction and a certain amount of nodding and head shaking and then the sergeant beckoned him over.

'Okay, son, why don't we see what you've got in your pockets?'

If Nick thought of refusing, standing there with three men staring at him soon wiped any such ideas from his mind. Besides, aside from his keys and some small change, a few scraps of paper, what would they find?

'There's nothing else?'

Nick shook his head.

'You're sure?'

'Yes.'

A bit more hushed discussion and he was told to go back and sit down.

'How much longer've I got to stay here?' Nick asked.

Nobody answered.

The two officers who had brought him in went away and after a short while he was aware of some movement in the corridor outside and faces looking at him through the square of glass at the top of the door.

Then nothing: nothing specific. The life of the station went on around him.

After what seemed an age but was probably no more than minutes, an officer he hadn't seen before approached. 'Best come wait in here.'

'I thought I could go.'

The room was small and airless, narrow, a table and several chairs. It smelt faintly of disinfectant.

'Lucky lad,' the officer said. 'Your mum's coming to get you.'

Nick closed his eyes.

★   ★   ★

Flustered, short of breath after running from the bus stop, Dawn excused herself past an African woman with a vibrant blue head-dress to get the duty officer's attention.

'Yes, ma'am?' He blinked back at her through reinforced glass.

'My son was brought here. Nick. Nick Harman. I was asked to come.'

'And you are?'

'I'm his mother. Mrs Harman. Dawn.'

'Just one moment.'

The officer turned aside, dialled a number and spoke into the phone.

'If you'll just wait here, someone will be out to see you.'

Dawn stepped aside and let the African woman past. Several others had entered and were milling around the entrance. Dawn glanced at her watch and shook her head and realised that what she wanted most was a cigarette.

The door from the interior of the station swung open and if she'd been expecting to see Nick she was mistaken.

'Mrs Harman?'

The woman holding out a hand was perhaps an inch taller than Dawn, dark hair cut short and framing a strong face that, a touch of lipstick aside, seemed free of make up. She was wearing a dark suit, brown with a thin stripe, jacket undone, trousers slightly flared. Late thirties, Dawn thought, a few years younger than herself.

'Jackie Ferris. Detective Inspector.' Her hand was smooth, its grip quick and strong. 'Let's go inside, shall we? Where we can talk.'

'I want to see my son.'

'Of course.'

Dawn followed her along a corridor and towards a flight of stairs.

Conversations, some ordered and calm, others less so, went on behind partitioned walls.

'With your permission, Mrs Harman, we'd like to ask your son some questions.'

'What about? What's he supposed to have done?'

Ferris stopped and turned. 'There was a robbery earlier this evening, around the time your son was on his way home. A group of youths attacked a man, four or five of them, and knocked him to the ground. Stole his wallet, watch, mobile phone.'

Dawn stared at her, incredulous. 'And you're saying Nick was involved?'

'Not necessarily, no.'

'Not necessarily . . .'

'Someone saw the tail end of what happened and called us. We had a couple of cars in the area. One of them drove round with the victim to see if he could pick out any of his attackers.'

'And he picked Nick?'

'Your boy was of a similar height and build and wearing similar clothes . . .'

'So's half the estate . . .'

'Mrs Harman, a search was carried out at the station with your son's consent.'

'And?'

'And we found nothing compromising, nothing . . .'

'Then why are you keeping him here like some criminal?'

'As I say, we'd like to ask him a few straight-forward questions in your presence. If he agrees.'

'And if he doesn't?'

The inspector waited just a fraction longer before replying. 'Then, of course, he can leave.'

Nick had been alternately sitting and pacing around, wondering how much longer he was going to kept there, running over and over in his mind what had happened. Whenever he heard footsteps approaching, he looked expectantly towards the door but the steps always continued on past.

A burglary. A mugging.

The two youths who had pushed past him at the alley's end, legging it for all they were worth.

He thought again about the one he might have recognised, uncertain.

The face he'd seen for a moment, little more.

This kid a year below him at school, skinny and tall.

If it was him, Nick had spotted him hanging round the estate, sometimes with Blevitt and his crew, sometimes not.

He was doing his best to fix on a name when he realised that this time the footsteps had stopped outside the door. Some woman he didn't know came in first and then his mum.

'Nick. Nicky. Are you all right?'

Dawn had to stop herself rushing forward and hugging him, knowing it would be the last thing he wanted. He'd not forgive her for embarrassing him.

'Yeah. Yeah, I'm okay.'

'You're sure?'

'Yeah.'

The inspector identified herself to Nick and said there were a few things she wanted to ask.

'I don't know nothin',' Nick said.

'Why don't we all sit down? This needn't take very long.'

Still Dawn hesitated, trying to read the expression on Nick's face, wondering if it was all as harmless as the detective was saying. Maybe she should have contacted a solicitor or something instead of doing this on her own? She didn't know what kinds of trouble Nick might talk himself into if he were given the chance.

'Mrs Harman? The sooner we're done, the sooner you can both be on your way.'

Dawn sat down.

Ferris began by confirming Nick's age and address and where he went to school, Nick not really looking her in the eye.

'And your father, Nick, is he living with you?'

Nick stared back at her then. 'My father's dead.'

'I'm sorry.'

34

'He jumped off a bridge, right? Jumped off some fucking bridge.' He felt tears pricking at the corners of his eyes and shook his head, wiped a hand across his face. He'd rather die than cry in front of her.

Dawn sat frozen in her chair, not knowing what to do.

'Would you like to take a few minutes?' Ferris asked. 'A drink of water?'

Nick shook his head.

Ferris took her time all the same, waiting for the tension to seep away. 'Were you aware of anything going on this evening when you were on your way home? Anything out of the ordinary?'

Nick shook his head again.

'A man was mugged. He'd been cutting through the same alley as you.'

Calm now, Nick looked back at her.

'What's that got to do with me?'

'The youths who attacked him, they would have run off in your direction. The direction you were walking.'

'I told you, I didn't see nothin'.'

There was a slight shift in his tone that Dawn recognised and she wondered if the inspector did too.

'You're sure?'

'Yeah, I'm sure.'

'You didn't see anyone at all?'

Rawlings, it came to him now. The youth who'd pushed past him. Rawlings. He'd heard them calling his name. Steve, he thought it might be. Steve. Steve Rawlings.

'No,' Nick said.

'And there's nothing else you can tell me?' the inspector said.

Nick shook his head. 'Can we go now?' he said, looking at his mother.

Dawn pushed back her chair. 'He's said he didn't see anything. He can't help you.'

Ferris nodded, took a card from her pocket and slid it across the table. 'If you do think of anything, give me a call.'

Glancing at the card, Nick wanted to leave it where it was, but instead be picked it up and pushed it down into the back pocket of his jeans.

'If you were protecting a friend, I could understand it,' Ferris said. 'But whoever this was, I don't think they're friends of yours.'

Nick didn't reply.

CHAPTER 6

Neither of them spoke all the way home.

As soon as they were inside the flat, Nick went to his room and closed the door.

Dawn didn't know what to do. She wanted to talk to him, but she didn't think Nick would want to speak to her. And if he did, she was half afraid of what he'd say.

Answering the inspector's questions – *You didn't see anything?* – she was sure Nick had lied but didn't know why.

As for the outburst about his father, well, it shouldn't have surprised her that after she'd given him the photos and everything, his dad should be on Nick's mind. But for him to come out with that the way he did, then and there, it made her realise how much she underestimated what it would make him feel. How angry.

Nick sat on his bed. An old CD by Aphex Twin was playing on the stereo. When Scott had first started going with Laura, he'd started listening to all that spacey, ambient kind of stuff, but unlike Laura it had proved a bit of a five minute wonder and Nick had reaped the rewards. *Selected Ambient Works Vol 2, Drukqs, Twenty Six Mixes for Cash.* Brian Eno's *Apollo* and *My Life in the Bush of Ghosts.* How far round the estate would the fact he'd been picked up by the police have gone? How far would it go round school?

He leaned back and closed his eyes.

When the music finished he remained where he was, unmoving, allowing the small sounds to gather round him.

The box containing his father's things was on the floor beside the bed, the lid askew, and he reached down and picked it up, sliding the lid back into place.

He wasn't going to let it screw him up.

If he shunted some things aside, there was just room for it in the drawer with his t-shirts and socks and stuff.

He could hear his mother now, crossing from the living room to the kitchen, the quick flow of water into the kettle.

'Hey, mum!' he called, easing open the door. 'There anything to eat?'

Dawn had checked that Nick didn't mind pizza twice in one day before phoning for a delivery. One American Hot with pepperoni and extra anchovies, one Hawaiian with pineapple and ham. Coleslaw and a large portion of garlic bread.

38

Pepsi and Seven Up. They sat in the kitchen, eating from the open boxes. Just this past twenty-four hours the weather had changed and it was warm enough to have the window partly open, traffic noises drifting in from the street outside.

Dawn had just finished telling Nick about the acoustic night in Highbury, the first time she had seen his dad.

It didn't seem possible that it was more than twenty years ago.

Not until she looked at Nick sitting there, all but fully grown, almost a man.

'You knew you were going to see him again then?'

'Not really.'

'You took his flier. Where he was going to be playing. You said so.'

'That didn't mean . . .'

'It meant you fancied him.'

'Not necessarily.'

'Oh, yeah. The music, was it? The way he played his guitar.'

'Don't be so cheeky.'

'You thought he was well fit.'

Smiling a little, Dawn bit into a piece more pizza. 'Maybe I did.'

'Where d'you see him next then?' Nick asked. 'Go on.'

'This place over in west London. Earls Court. The Troubadour. It was famous, apparently.

That kind of music. Bob Dylan had played there. All kinds of people. Paul Simon. It was just a cellar really, underneath a coffee bar, but your dad liked it, he played there quite a bit.'

She paused for a mouthful of Seven Up.

Nick folded a triangle of pizza back on itself and bit into it, catching a spiral of stray cheese with his finger and winding it back up.

'He recognised me the moment I walked in, though, of course, he didn't let on.'

'You went on your own?'

'No. I dragged this mate of mine along.'

'Not the one who was after him?'

Dawn laughed. 'You think I'm stupid?'

No, Nick didn't think that. 'So what happened?'

'He took his time, finally came over and said, "How about that drink then?", something like that. I said 'All right,' and he said, 'Coffee, then,' and I must have made a face, I didn't like coffee much at the time. Turned out the place wasn't licensed, it was pretty much coffee or nothing, so we went upstairs and sat at one of these small tables.' She smiled. 'Must have been my first cappuccino. We chatted for a bit, don't ask me what about. I was looking round half the time. Some right types. Arty, you know. A lot of black jumpers. People sitting around reading, playing chess.'

Nick tried to imagine it, not quite succeeding.

'When Les went back down to play,' his mum continued, 'he broke a string right in the middle of

40

the first number. I thought it would throw him off, but no, he told this story while he was fitting a new string, about the time he'd been playing with a couple of American blues musicians. One of them, Sonny Terry, he was blind, and Les, it was quite a big thing for him so he'd been drinking more than usual, more than he should, and somehow they got locked, the pair of them, inside the dressing room. Stumbling around, falling over things, trying to get out. The blind drunk, as Les said, leading the blind.

'People laughed, of course, and by then he was ready and he went right back on with the song. And I really admired that, the way he seemed so at ease, didn't matter where he was or what size the audience, up there in front of a microphone, he was so confident, sure of himself.'

She stopped and turned her head away and Nick thought she was probably crying.

'What?' he asked. 'What is it?'

Her voice was so quiet he had to strain to hear.

'The last time I went with him, somewhere just out of London, Hitchin I think it was, he couldn't even get his guitar out of its case, never mind get up on stage.'

'Because he'd been drinking?' Nick said.

'Because he was afraid.'

'What of?'

'Everything. Not being any good, people not liking him. Everything.'

* * *

41

There were a hundred more questions Nick wanted to ask, but his mum had made it clear enough was enough. Some other time maybe, but even then he couldn't be sure. As if there were things she didn't want to talk about, places she didn't want to go.

They said good night and for the first time in a long while she kissed him, fleetingly, on the cheek, her face just brushing his.

'G'night, mum,' Nick said again and went into his room.

There was reading he had to do, history. More stuff about the Nazis, the rise of Hitler, the Second World War. As if nothing else had ever happened. Scott's eldest brother had been taken prisoner in Iraq. The Gulf War. Most days he walked the streets and when you spoke to him, he looked away. Scott said some nights he wet the bed, just like a kid. How come they never learned about that?

After quarter of an hour Nick realised he'd read the same page four times without taking in a thing.

Opening the drawer, he took out the box and from the box took out the audio cassette. Slotting it down into the tape deck of the stereo he pressed play.

A hiss and then the notes of a guitar.

Nick lay back on his bed and suddenly there was his father's voice, surprisingly light and high.

Woke up this morning, towel round my head,
Woke up this morning, towel round my head,
Looked in the mirror, wished that I were dead.

His turn to cry.

CHAPTER 7

Next day, Nick came straight home after school.

Christopher was meeting his cousin or something up in Finchley and Scott had gone back to Laura's – both her parents worked and her sister was staying late for netball. Scott had been scrounging money to buy some rubbers. And Nick had work to do on his art project, which had started off brilliantly, but then got stalled.

'You've got a real chance for an A in this,' his Art teacher had told him. 'You know that, don't you?'

Nick had shrugged and examined the floor. An A in anything would be good, and this was about the only chance he had.

'Well, you best pull your finger out then. Time's getting on.'

Nick nodded and dragged out a 'Yes, sir.'

To begin with, using a borrowed camera, he had taken pictures of some of the market stalls in Holloway and Kentish Town. Some of the stall owners had been happy to pose for him, holding up bunches of bananas, packets of men's underpants,

44

three for a pound, wrapping paper with last year's Christmas design. He'd photographed the giant boots and shoes that hung above the half a million shoe stores that littered Camden High Street.

The best of these he had arranged and pasted painstakingly down on to sheets of different coloured paper, interleaved with blown-up copies of the appropriate pages from the A–Z.

The trouble was, he couldn't really see what to do next.

He had tried painting street scenes, working from memory and a few sketches he had hurriedly made, but each time he opened his folder and looked at them he had to resist the temptation to tear them into small pieces and throw them away.

The project needed something, though, what he had on its own was not enough. He was thinking about this, not getting anywhere, when he saw Melanie Mitchell cutting across the path ahead of him, heavily-laden bags from Iceland in each hand.

Melanie lived in the same block of flats, on the top floor; her mum was a dinner lady at one of the local primary schools, and her dad worked on the post and seemed to spend most of his afternoons in the betting shop or the pub. When Nick had been a lot younger, he and Melanie had played together quite a bit, their mums chatting while they took turns to push them on the roundabouts and swings. Picnicking on the bandstand in Parliament Hill Fields.

But then, a little older, Nick had only wanted to play with boys, charging around after a football and coming home with scuffed shoes and grazed knees, and he hardly saw Melanie at all.

By the time they got to junior school, what had been chubbiness in Melanie had turned to fat and other children, Nick included, laughed at her and shouted names, poked at her with sticks, and gave cruel impressions of the way she wobbled when she walked, a jelly on a plate.

At eleven she and Nick went to different schools and not long after that he remembered his mum telling him Melanie had been sent to a special unit with some kind of eating disorder. She was thin and then she was fat again, fatter than before.

'Don't you ever let me hear you say anything,' his mum had said. 'Don't you ever dare.'

Today, walking slowly along the path towards the flats, bags of shopping in each hand, Melanie was fat. No two ways about it.

Nick slowed his pace, letting her reach the forecourt ahead of him but then realised he'd have to wait forever while she negotiated the main door. Giving her a wide berth, he hurried ahead and was just reaching for his keys when he heard a crash and a shout and turned to see Melanie surrounded by the contents of one of her bags, some of them still rolling in slow small circles away from where she stood.

Even from that distance he could see the tears in her eyes.

The keys were cold and shiny in his hand, the door at his back.

'Here,' he said. 'Hang on. I'll give you a hand.'

'No, it's all right. It doesn't matter. I can manage.' Not looking him in the eye.

A jar of strawberry jam had smashed, as had a bottle of HP sauce, and heaven knew what the eggs were like inside their grey cardboard box.

Nick retrieved the first of several tins of baked beans which had rolled some distance away and set it down next to a swiss roll and a frozen Sara Lee Danish Apple Bar. Melanie had put down her other bags and was bending towards the ground.

'The handles,' she said, 'they snapped.'

'Maybe we can still use the bag,' Nick said. 'I'll carry it upstairs for you.'

'My mum,' Melanie said, 'she'll go spare.'

'It wasn't your fault.'

Close to, around the mouth and nose and eyes, her face was actually quite pretty, Nick realised.

'Hey, get a look at this,' came a voice from the corner of the building. 'Nick and his girl friend've been shopping.'

Over Melanie's shoulder, Nick could see Ross Blevitt and four or five of his entourage.

'Settin' up house together, Nicky?'

'Shackin' up.'

'Knocked her up, eh, Nick?'

Melanie's neck was burning red and her hands were starting to shake.

47

'Ignore them,' Nick said, and continued, purposefully, to load up the broken bag.

'Nick wouldn't fancy that, would you, Nick?' It was Blevitt himself now, pushing his way through his crew, a hundred pounds worth or more of Adidas trainers at the end of his skinny but expensive Aquascutum trousers. 'Not without a compass and a torch to find the hole.'

'Shut it, Blevitt!' Nick said.

Silence closed around his words.

For some moments, nobody moved and then, slowly, Blevitt started towards Nick, staring at him all the while, not stopping until he was close enough to swing his fists at his face. Except Nick knew the last time Blevitt had got into a fight it hadn't just been fists he'd used.

A sixteen year old from east London, Walthamstow, had come over to watch a game at Highbury with his mates and made the mistake of hanging around. He and Blevitt had got into an argument and Blevitt had left three stripes across his face, after which some of his crew had laced into him with their boots and a length of chain.

'Maybe I didn't hear right,' Blevitt said. 'Just now.'

Nick said nothing.

'Pussy!' called someone and then it echoed round. 'Pussy, pussy.'

'Not so big now,' Blevitt said. 'Not like your girl friend here.'

'I told you to shut your mouth,' Nick said, even and quiet.

Blevitt's eyes narrowed and his body tensed.

'Don't, Nick. He's not worth it,' Melanie said.

Blevitt's head angled towards her in surprise. 'Keep out of this, you fat slag.'

Nick knew that was his chance, get in first, strike the first blow.

A first floor window opened with a bang and an old man's bony head poked out, white hair fluffy and unkempt around the ears. 'You lot. Whatever this is, take it elsewhere.'

'Hey, Granddad!' someone shouted. 'Get back in your cage.'

'And you, Nick Harman,' the old man said, pointing. 'I'd've thought better of you.'

Nick knew him a little, ex-army, forever trying to talk his mum into joining the Neighbourhood Watch.

'Now clear off the lot of you before I phone the police.'

'Talking of the police,' Blevitt said, moving even closer to Nick, ignoring the old man's rant. 'I hear they picked you up. Suspicion of robbery.' He smiled with his eyes. 'Mistaken identity. Got to be.'

'Yeah,' Nick said. 'Maybe they thought I was you.'

Blevitt laughed. 'I got better things to do.' And then, 'You didn't tell 'em nothing?'

'What d'you think?'

Blevitt studied Nick's face then stepped away. 'Come on,' he said. 'We're out of here.'

A minute or so later, they were gone. The first floor window closed and the lace curtains were quickly drawn across. Nick pushed the last few items down into the broken bag and lifted it under one arm, picking up one of the other bags with his free hand.

'You didn't need to do that,' Melanie said.

He wasn't sure if she meant retrieve the shopping or stand up to Ross Blevitt.

'Let's get this inside,' he said. 'I've got stuff to do.'

When the door to Melanie's flat opened the sound of the television was loud from inside. 'What's all this then?' Melanie's mother said.

Nick thought it was obvious enough.

He set the broken bag down on the floor alongside the rest.

'Thanks, Nick,' Melanie said.

Nick nodded and headed for the stairs. He'd have liked to think Blevitt would be content to leave things as they were, but he doubted if it were true.

CHAPTER 8

'What the hell got into you, man?'
They were sitting an unsteady table out in front of the café, early lunchtime Friday, kids pressing round them, Nick, Scott and Christopher, one slice of pizza apiece. While they were talking, Scott was busy texting Laura, even though she was only across the street.

'You got a death wish all of a sudden?' Christopher said.

'You're talking bollocks,' Nick said.

'Oh, yeah?'

'Stick to *Play Station*,' Scott said. '*Splinter Cell*. Lose your head that way.'

'I'm not afraid of Ross Blevitt.'

'Blevitt, maybe not,' said Christopher. 'On his own. But Blevitt plus that bunch of Neanderthals he hangs with.'

'Look,' Nick said. 'Nothing happened.'

'Yet,' said Scott. 'You forget "yet".'

'Jesus!'

'He's right,' Christopher said. 'Blevitt's not going to leave it there.'

'Yeah, well we can, right? So just shut up about it.'

Grabbing his piece of pizza, Nick grated his chair round until he was looking away from his friends and out across the street. And there was Steve Rawlings, can of drink in his hand, mouthing off to a bunch of his mates. Rawlings wearing the same top, hood up, as he had when he had raced out of the alley two nights before.

Stay cool, Nick told himself. You don't want to get involved.

But Rawlings had recognised him and was nudging his mates and jerking his head in Nick's direction. Grinning and giving him the finger. Not caring who saw.

'Hang on here,' Nick said, getting to his feet.

'Where you going?'

'Nick, what's up?'

Slipping between the traffic, Nick crossed to where Rawlings was standing, close to the pavement's edge.

'Want somethin'?' Rawlings said, cocky as they come.

Nick caught hold of Rawlings' arm, hard above the elbow. 'You think it's funny, what happened the other night? Yeah?'

Rawlings tried to shake himself free and failed, his friends milling round, waiting to see what would happen next.

'Down the police station, on account of you.'

'Leggo my arm.'

Nick tightened his grip. 'I'll tell you what,' he said. 'Maybe next time I'll tell them what they want to know. Okay?' He pressed harder against the arm, fingers bearing down against the bone. 'Okay?'

'Yeah, yeah. You say.'

'And if you stick your finger up at me again, I'll break it off and shove it up your arse.'

One of Rawlings' friends sniggered and abruptly Nick released his grip and turned away, Rawlings shouting something in his wake as Nick walked briskly back across the street.

'God! What was all that about?' Laura asked, having left her friends and hurried across.

'Nothing,' Nick said, pulling his chair back round to the table and sitting down.

Laura looked questioningly at Scott, who merely shrugged.

'Here,' Christopher said, pushing what was left of his pizza in Nick's direction. 'If you're turning yourself into Steven Seagal you'd better bulk out fast.'

A little way off, one of Ross Blevitt's lieutenants was watching everything with more than a little interest.

Finishing Friday afternoon with English wasn't too bad as far as Nick was concerned. Most of the time he could just sit there, half taking in whatever was going on around him while thinking about the weekend, what he might be doing. Christopher was going off to spend time with his mum and sister in Oxford, but Scott was going to be around, maybe they'd meet up Saturday afternoon, go down Camden, even if it meant Laura tagging along. Saturday evening, Sunday lunchtime he was working.

Nick realised the teacher was looking at him, asking him a question.

The book they were doing, *The Grapes of Wrath*, was about migrant farmers trekking half way across America to look for work. On the way there some of them died or just gave up and then when they arrived they were stuck into camps and made to work long hours for almost no pay. Asylum seekers of their day, the teacher had said, maybe it helps to think of them that way. Economic migrants.

The question Nick was being asked now seemed to have more to do with Geography than anything and he tried faking an answer until what he was saying sounded stupid even to himself and he stopped mid-sentence and slumped back in his seat. Immediately, some wise ass at the back started on about top soil and irrigation and Nick could see from the teacher's face that was the answer he'd been wanting.

A/B was what he'd been forecast for English, but that had been last term and most of his grades recently had been C at best.

English and Maths, Nick, his mum kept on at him. That's what you're going to need if you're going to get a good job, English and Maths.

54

Nick shuffled a few pages of the book and glanced at his watch. The teacher was pulling down the screen over the blackboard and asking someone over by the wall to get the lights.

'I want you to look carefully at these slides, reproductions of photographs taken at roughly the same time the book is set.'

More often than not, to an ironic cheer, the first slide came on upside down or back to front or both, but this time it was fine.

'Dorothea Lange,' the teacher said, and because he no longer had access to the board, he spelt it out for them. 'That's Dorothea with a "ea" and Lange with an "e" at the end. Most of her photographs, those that concern us anyway, were taken in the nineteen-thirties during the Depression.'

Nick was staring at the black and white picture of a man behind the wheel of a truck or van; under his cap the man's face is triangular and thin and his eyes are large and staring out as if he's frightened, perhaps, of what he sees. And yes, Nick thought, it reminded him of refugees he'd seen on the news, the ones from eastern Europe somewhere, Moldova or Romania, the ones who would cling on to the underside of the Eurostar train to get across the Channel or risk being packed like sardines in the back of a lorry, half-suffocating. It even reminded him a little of men he saw outside the tube at Camden Town, begging, sleeping rough.

'*Ditched, Stalled and Stranded*,' the teacher said.

'That's what this photograph was called. California, 1935.'

The next slides showed a succession of similar images: men squatting at the edges of muddy fields or outside a corner store; men lying in the street or crowding round a soup kitchen; men walking with their possessions along flat, dusty roads.

'And these,' the teacher said, 'are probably Dorothea Lange's most famous photographs, two of a series of six that she took in 1936 of the same woman and her children living in a makeshift tent. The woman had just sold the tyres from her car for food.'

In the first picture the woman's eyes were half-closed, her shirt part-open, a young child pressed up against her breast; in the second, closer, the young child is asleep and two others, toddlers, are leaning on her shoulders, backs to the camera, while her mother rests her head on her hand.

'How old,' the teacher said, 'do you think this woman is?'

'Sixty,' came the first voice.

'Don't be stupid,' said another. 'What about the baby? She's got a baby.'

'All right, then. Fifty.'

'Fifty-five.'

'Forty-seven.'

'When those shots were taken,' the teacher said, 'the woman in them was just thirty-two.'

He signalled and the lights came back on, the

image disappeared. 'When you're reading,' the teacher said, 'and thinking about the characters, I want you to keep those photographs in mind.'

People fidgeted in their chairs and small conversations started. It was near to the end of the lesson, the end of the day. Nick glanced inside the back of his book where he'd written Dorothea Lange's name and flicked it shut.

CHAPTER 9

What had someone said about Camden Market? After the Tower and Madame Tussaud's, it was the biggest tourist attraction in London.

That afternoon, Nick could believe it.

Walking with Scott and Laura, the crowd spreading over the pavements and into the road, it was more or less impossible for them to stick together, three abreast. Most of the visitors were young, not much older than themselves, and from the criss-cross of languages that volleyed about them, mostly foreign. Aside from the Goths, that is. Nick didn't know why, but he assumed most of the Goths were English. Maybe he couldn't imagine them travelling by plane or ferry wearing the whole black outfit, the gear, their hair sometimes shaped and gelled into extravagant Mohicans and every available part of their body hanging with silver rings and crucifixes. Dark purple lipstick. High boots with pointed toes.

'Nick! Nick! Over here.'

He elbowed his way to where Scott and Laura

were standing in a small queue at one of several stalls selling Chinese food.

'You want anything?'

Nick shook his head. He'd cooked himself some pasta at lunchtime, the sort that was ready in three minutes, slathered it over with a jar of tomato-and-something sauce. Two scoops of ice cream from the freezer for desert. His mum would moan like crazy about the fact he'd left the washing up, but, as he liked to point out, where washing up was concerned he was now a professional and expected to be paid.

Scott came away with a portion of chicken chow mien and a spring roll.

'I reckon you've got worms,' Laura said, lighting a cigarette.

'I hope not,' Scott said, 'for your sake.'

Laura made a face. 'Gross!'

They made their way between the lines of outdoor stalls, heading for the covered section near the canal. One of Laura's friends had found a great miniskirt down here a few weeks before, a real bargain, and Scott had half an eye out for a new game for his PS2, maybe even a knock-off *Rainbow Six 3: Raven Shield*.

Music blurred, distorted, from all directions: 50 Cent, Bob Dylan, Queen.

Nick lingered a while over some CDs and then, on the further edge, spotted a display of postcards outside a small shop selling posters and frames.

'Hey, Scott! I'll be over here.'

Scott gave him the thumbs up.

More than half of the cards were black and white, portraits, many of them, of people like Marilyn Monroe and Marlon Brando, James Dean, jazz musicians Nick didn't know. And then, turning the display, he saw the top half of an image he immediately recognised.

Migrant Mother, Nipomo, California, 1936.

Carefully, Nick lifted it up and into the light.

It was the second of the photographs they'd been shown in class, the one with the baby sleeping and the other children huddled close.

Setting the card aside, Nick went back through the rest. He was hoping he might find the picture of the man at the wheel – what was it? *Ditched, Stranded and Stalled* – but found instead a picture of a farmhouse in the middle of a vast, ploughed field.

Nick turned it over and looked at the back: *Tractored Out*, Childress County, Texas, 1938. Dorothea Lange.

He took the two cards to the man sitting inside reading.

'How much?'

'One sixty.'

'How much?'

'One sixty.'

'You're taking the piss.'

'You don't want 'em, put 'em back,' the man said and turned the page in his book.

Reluctantly, Nick took the money from his

pocket and, without comment, the man put the cards in a brown paper bag.

Nick went outside to look for Scott and Laura.

'What've you been buying?' a voice said and for a moment Nick couldn't see who was speaking.

It was Ellen.

'Oh, nothing,' Nick said, glancing down at the bag as the colour flooded his cheeks. 'Just a couple of cards, that's all.'

'You on your own?'

'Yes. I mean, no. No. Scott and . . . I'm with Scott, Scott and Laura.'

Nick looked vaguely out into the crowd.

Ellen smiled the suggestion of a smile.

'You?' Nick forced himself to ask.

Ellen nodded. 'I was going to get some coffee,' she said.

'Okay, I . . .'

'Just over there.'

The queue was long enough but the service was fast and Nick stood alongside Ellen as they shuffled forward, wishing he could think of something to say. Doing his best not to stare.

'Let's go over here,' she said once they'd been served, pointing in the direction of the canal, and Nick followed her, glancing round from time to time to see if either Scott or Laura were anywhere in sight.

They sat on a low wall, balancing their cups on the brick's rough curve.

Ellen was wearing a lavender blue shirt, loose

61

over a white t-shirt and blue jeans. Nick, in his grubby Levi's and last season's replica Arsenal shirt, wished he was wearing something smarter, something else.

'How come you're not there?'

'Um?'

'Highbury.'

'Oh,' Nick said and left it at that. He went two or three times a season at best. Christopher had Sky – that and just about everything else – and Nick would watch whenever he got the chance.

'My dad's got a season ticket,' Ellen said. 'Spurs.'

'Never mind,' Nick said and grinned.

A boat passed through the lock and made its way slowly along the canal towards Regent's Park.

'What did you get?' Ellen asked, looking at the brown bag now resting by Nick's foot.

'Like I said, just a couple of cards.'

'Aren't you going to let me see?'

Reaching down, Nick passed the bag across.

'Dorothea Lange,' Ellen said, the moment she saw the cards. 'Both of them, right?'

Nick nodded.

'I love her stuff. Even though most of it's pretty fake.'

'What d'you mean?'

'Well . . .' She held up one of the cards. '. . . this one, for instance. You think it's dead real, right? Authentic. But it's posed. And then the way she crops the frame . . .'

'Crops?'

'To get the best composition.'

Nick shook his head. 'I like it.'

'Of course you do. It's great. Iconic. Just not what it seems.'

If she weren't so good looking, Nick thought, he'd push her into the canal.

'I'm sorry,' Ellen said, reading his face. 'I just went on this course. Last weekend. *Realism and Twentieth Century Photography*. It was great. Well, some of it was great. Actually a lot of it was boring and there was some I didn't understand at all.'

'So why did you go?'

'It's what I want to do.'

'Be a photographer?'

Ellen shook her head. 'Be a curator, in a gallery. Tate Modern, somewhere like that.'

Nick wondered if a curator was anything like a caretaker and decided probably it wasn't.

'How old are you?' he asked.

'Sixteen, why?'

He grinned. 'Just checking, that's all.' Sixteen and it was as though she had her life planned out, whereas he didn't know what he wanted to be doing next week.

'You think I'm weird, don't you?' Ellen said.

Nick was shrewd enough to know the answer was supposed to be yes.

'No,' he said. 'Not at all.'

'Hey!' Scott's voice came from over Nick's shoulder. 'So this is where you are.'

Immediately, Nick felt himself blushing. Again.

'Hi, Ellen,' said Laura.

'Hello, Laura.'

For a long moment, no one said anything. Then Ellen swung her legs down from the wall.

'I've got to be going. See you. Bye.'

And with scarcely a second glance at Nick she was walking away, down onto the tow path and out of sight.

'How long's that been going on?' Scott said.

'What?'

'You and her.'

'Bollocks. There's nothing going on.'

'Not what it looked like to me,' Laura said.

'Yeah, well. We were just chatting, that's all.'

'Sure,' Laura said with a smug little grin.

'So what's she like?' Scott asked a few minutes later.

'Weird,' Nick said. 'And too clever by half. Or at least she thinks she is. And her old man's a Spurs supporter.'

'That's it then. Over before it's begun.'

The busier it was at work, the more Nick liked it. For one thing the time went faster. For another, if he kept up, if he even, for a while at least, kept ahead of the game, well, it made him feel as though he'd achieved something. It made him feel good.

This evening, though, had started off like a hurricane. He hardly seemed to have rolled up his sleeves when Marcus was shouting for clean plates and the pile of unwashed ones waiting to be scraped was leaning like the Tower of Pisa. Cutlery was strewn haphazardly everywhere and the chef was breaking Nick's balls for letting a small pan get back onto the stove with a residue of sauce still clinging to the sides.

Nick ran fresh water, scalding hot.

The kitchen radio was tuned to Kiss FM and the restaurant stereo was playing Norah Jones. Midway through the evening. Marcus yanked him away from the sink and tossed a clean white coat in his direction.

'Go clear the deserts off that counter. I've got ice cream melting, bread and butter pudding getting cold.'

Thirty minutes later, it was: 'Nick, we're out of lemons. Run to that Costcutter on the corner. Beg, borrow or steal, okay?'

It was okay.

When, not so far short of one o'clock, Nick finally dumped his second apron of the evening on the floor and stretched his aching back, Marcus slipped an extra ten pound note into his pocket. 'You did good, kid. Go home.'

He was just coming out of the tunnel beneath the railway line when the brick struck him on the head. After that it was boots and fists and something that was either a baseball bat or a length of wood before they were running off, leaving him curled into a ball.

When he tried, gingerly, to get to his feet, his

legs crumpled beneath him and he crouched there on all fours, wincing each time he tried to breath.

And when he opened his eyes, the blood running down from the gash across his forehead meant that he couldn't see.

CHAPTER 10

By the time Nick finally made it home, half-crawling, half-staggering, it was close to two. Dawn had woken a short time before and, realising Nick was not yet back, put on her dressing gown and paced the kitchen, made a cup of tea. When she heard his key in the lock she smiled with relief and when she saw his face she had to stifle a scream.

'Oh, my God, Nick . . .'

His face was a mask of blood.

He took two uncertain paces into the narrow hall, leaving bloodied hand prints on the wall, before collapsing at her feet.

When the woman at the emergency services switchboard sought to assess the seriousness of the incident, Dawn left her in no doubt. Nick's breathing was rasping and raw and each breath made him wince with pain. In the short time before the ambulance arrived, Dawn bent low beside him, cautiously wiping his face with a flannel, assuring him everything would be all right.

One of the paramedics winked at Dawn as they

lifted him onto the trolley. 'Don't worry, sweet-heart. He'll be fine.'

In the ambulance, she held his hand and cried.

Accident and Emergency was crowded and noisy. Dirty. A man in clothes not much better than rags was swearing at the triage nurse, the same litany of words over and over again. Dawn feared they might be shunted off into a corner and left to wait but within minutes they were in one of several curtained cubicles and Dawn was helping a young male nurse lift Nick onto a narrow bed.

'The doctor won't be long.'

Dawn tried not to look at her watch.

When the doctor finally arrived she was small and harassed, stains on the front of a white coat which hung almost to the floor, the sleeves folded back. Australian, Dawn thought, when she heard her voice.

After a brief examination, the doctor ducked away again, promising she'd return. Above the hubbub of voices, the press of feet on the solid floor, Dawn heard the occasional shout raised in distress or anger, the occasional crash.

Nick lay scarcely moving, his breathing slightly easier now, head a little to one side, eyes closed.

Dawn was just pulling back the curtain to look for the doctor, when she reappeared.

'Help me turn him onto his side a moment, will you?'

Nick cried out as he was moved and Dawn felt her breath catch in her throat.

The doctor felt and listened.

'All right, he can lay back down.'

She leaned forward, examining the wound to Nick's head.

'He'll need stitches to the head. And we'll need to take him down to x-ray. I wouldn't be surprised if he hasn't got a couple of broken ribs. I'll have the nurse clean him up and apply a temporary dressing.' She smiled quickly. 'I'm afraid as usual we're pretty backed up.'

'He'll be all right?'

'Oh, yes. Strong boy like that. He'll be fine.' And she was gone.

Not so much later the nurse returned and began, using cotton wool and water, to wipe away the excess blood.

'Is it always like this?' Dawn asked.

The nurse grinned. 'Worse,' he said. 'A whole lot worse.'

The doctor who put the stitches in was Canadian, young, slowly making his way round the world; the nurse assisting him was West Indian, a large woman with big eyes and small, quick hands.

'He's a lucky boy,' the doctor said, drawing the last stitch.

'Really?' Dawn said.

'Another inch or so, he could have lost an eye.'

Nick stirred, winced, the effects of the local anaesthetic wearing off.

'Will there be a scar?' Dawn asked.

'We'll know better when the stitches come out,' the doctor said. 'But, yeah, a small one I'd say.'

'Don't worry,' the nurse said, resting a hand for a moment on Dawn's shoulder. 'He's still a good lookin' boy. This only make him more interestin' to the girls.'

With Dawn's help, she lifted him down and into a wheelchair.

'Tell him not to head the ball for a bit, okay,' the doctor said.

Nick said something that wasn't quite a word.

Two of Nick's ribs were broken. The bruises to his legs and back and arms would fade, the abrasions would heal over and disappear. The ribs would heal in time. How long it would be before he could step into the dark and then, without apprehension, back out into the light was anybody's guess.

'How are you feeling now?' Dawn asked.

'Like shit,' Nick said.

They were sitting near the main exit, waiting for a taxi to take them home.

'You still don't want to tell me what happened?' Dawn said.

'Someone threw a brick at me.'

'I know that much.'

'There you are then.'

'What about the rest?'

'What d'you want me to say? I got beaten up. Obviously.'

'But why? Who by?'

'It doesn't matter.'

'Of course it matters. Of course it bloody matters.'

Nick shook his head. 'Mum . . .'

'What?'

'Leave it, okay?'

Dawn sat back and looked at her watch. Almost a quarter past five. They had been at the hospital for close to three hours.

'I bet the other guy looks worse, eh?' the taxi driver said, holding open the door to his cab. Each time they went over one of the speed bumps in the road, Nick winced and held his breath.

Back home, Dawn gingerly helped Nick off with his clothes and into his bed.

'What can I get you? Tea? Coffee? Water? Hot chocolate, maybe.'

'Nothing. I'm fine.'

'You're sure?'

He didn't reply. Dawn left the door to his room ajar so as to be sure she'd hear him if he called. She hadn't realised, sitting in the hospital, how tired she felt herself. A cup of coffee would wake her up.

When she went back in to look at Nick some twenty minutes later, he was fast asleep on his back, head a little to one side, both arms spread wide. Sometimes, little more than a baby, he had slept curled inwards, clutching some small fluffy animal or other, and sometimes like this: defence-less, Dawn had always thought.

She wished she knew who'd done this to him, wanted them, more than anything, to get what they deserved. Bending low, she kissed Nick alongside the stitches to his head. As well, she thought, wish for the moon.

CHAPTER 11

Nick slept off and on for most the day and when he finally woke he had been hungry, ravenous, and demanded an egg and bacon sandwich – not an easy thing to eat in bed, especially when HP sauce is involved – and the evidence was clear at the corners of Nick's mouth and on the sheets. After that he wolfed down two slices of bread and apricot jam, a small black cherry yoghurt, several biscuits and an orange.

'Got your appetite back, at least,' Dawn said.

'Indian for dinner, right?' Nick said.

Dawn agreed, laughing. There'd been a time when they'd called the Bengal Spice on the Holloway Road every few weeks. Not the nearest but, to Dawn's mind, the best.

'Those photographs,' she said. 'The ones of your dad. I never got to see them.'

Nick nodded in the direction of the chest of drawers across the room. 'Second down, right hand side.'

Dawn spread them, slightly overlapping, across the bed, and after a while Nick rearranged them into chronological order, so that his father grew

73

older before his eyes. Never getting as old as Nick would have liked.

'See this,' Dawn said, pointing to a black and white photo which showed Nick's dad playing guitar, seated, while a woman sang, eyes closed, into a microphone. 'That's down the Troubadour. The place I told you about.'

'Where he pulled you.'

She looked back at him. 'Yes. If you like.'

'Who's she then?'

Dawn picked up the photograph. The singer was standing with one hand on the mike stand, the other arm thrown out wide, palm open, fingers spread. Her hair was dark and curly in a style then fashionable, nose strong and sharp, mouth wide, dark make-up around the closed eyes. She was wearing a long dress in what looked like crushed velvet, arms and shoulders bare. Nick's father's eyes were focussed on her to the exclusion of all else.

'Charlene. Charlene Bell. Charlie, that's what everyone called her.'

'And she was a singer?'

'So rumour had it.' There was no disguising the bite of sarcasm in Dawn's voice.

'She sang with my dad?'

'Sometimes.'

'And?'

'What d'you mean?'

'You know what I mean.'

'Do I?'

'You don't like her.'

Dawn shook her head. 'It was a long time ago.'

'You didn't like her then.'

'Actually, that's not true. I liked her quite a lot. She didn't suffer fools gladly, Charlie, which was no bad thing. Those days especially. No, she was okay. She was good to me. We had a laugh together.'

'And my dad? What did he think of her?'

'She was a good singer. That kind of stuff, blues, you know.'

'That's not what I meant.'

'Ah, well,' Dawn said, 'I dare say.' Dropping the photograph back on the bed, she got to her feet. 'I think I fancy a cup of tea, how about you?'

Nick nodded okay. He waited until his mother was out of the room and looked at the photo again, at Charlie, Charlene, trying to see her with his father's eyes.

'She's still around, you know,' Dawn said, putting her head back round the door. 'I'm sure I've seen her name from time to time.'

'Singing, you mean?'

'I imagine so. You want another biscuit with this or can you hold on till your Rogon Josh?'

'Where've you seen her?'

'Oh, I dunno. That pub down Kentish Town, near Nandos. Went Irish and changed it's name. You know? They used to have an acoustic night, upstairs. I saw her name in the window a few times.'

'You never went in?'

She looked at him. 'No point in getting it all stirred up again.'

'Then why tell me?'

Dawn gestured towards the opened box, the photos on the bed. 'He obviously wanted you to have all this stuff. Know what it was he did, music and that. Charlie, she worked with him. I mean, I was around for some of it, towards the end. But Charlie, she knew him early on.'

'And you think I should talk to her? Try and see her?'

'I don't know. It depends.'

'On what?'

'How much you want to, I suppose. How much you want to know.'

'And you don't mind?'

Dawn shook her head. 'He was your dad.' She smiled, all but her eyes. 'I'll get the tea.'

The next day Christopher and Scott came to see him after school.

'Where's the grapes, then?' Nick said.

Scott shook his head. 'We got you ice cream instead. Ben and Jerry's Rocky Road.'

Nick's favourite, as they knew. 'So what've you done with it?' he asked. 'Stuck it in the fridge?'

'No,' Scott said. 'You kidding? We ate it on the way here.'

'You're lying.'

'We're not.'

'Bastards, then.'

'It was great, wasn't it?' Scott said, turning to Christopher. 'Just starting to melt. The best.'

Nick threw a pillow at him and gasped at the sudden pain, sharp in his side. He'd thought they might have bandaged his chest or something, but no, best apparently to let his ribs heal by themselves. Not too much time in bed, either, that's what the nurse had said. No lounging around. He had painkillers for when it got too bad.

'Are you okay?' Christopher said, concerned.

'Do I look as if I'm okay?'

'You look like shit.'

'Thanks a lot.'

'Well, you do.'

'So what happened?' Christopher asked, sitting on the side of the bed.

Nick shook his head.

'We're your mates,' Scott said. 'You've got to tell us.'

'If you were my mates, you'd wouldn't have scarfed the ice cream.'

'We were just having you on,' Christopher said. 'It's in the kitchen.'

'Straight up?'

'Straight up. Now tell us what happened.'

Nick told them as well as he could, what little he knew.

'They were waiting for you,' Scott said.

'Looks like.'

'And they didn't take anything?'

Nick shook his head. 'I had cash in my pockets, didn't I? Quite a bit.'

'It was Rawlings, then. Has to be. After you made him look stupid in front of his mates.'

'He wouldn't have the bottle,' Nick said.

'How much bottle does it take? Chucking a brick at someone when they're not looking.'

'I still don't reckon it was him. Not on his own, anyway.'

'This wasn't anyone on their own,' Scott said. 'We know that.'

'That's not what I mean,' Nick said.

They looked at him. 'You think it was Blevitt?' Christopher said.

Nick shrugged.

'Blevitt and Rawlings, they hang round together?'

'Sometimes.'

Christopher nodded. 'If it was him, Blevitt and his crew, what you gonna do about it?'

There was a knock on the door and Dawn came in holding a tray. 'I've got ice cream and Coke and Nick, you've got another visitor.'

Melanie was standing behind her, awkward in a denim skirt and loose blue top, a bunch of flowers in her hand. Tulips and daffodils.

'You can come in, Melanie,' Dawn said, setting down the tray. 'He won't bite.'

Christopher and Scott exchanged glances and quickly looked away before they burst out laughing.

Slowly Melanie moved closer and stood beside

78

the bed. 'I'm sorry about what happened, Nick. Really sorry. I thought you might like these.'

She held out the flowers and, blushing furiously, Nick said, 'Thanks. Thanks a lot.'

'Here, Melanie,' Dawn said, stepping forward. 'I'll take them and put them in some water.'

'Thanks, Mrs Harman.'

'Stay and have some ice cream. There's plenty to go round.'

'No, it's all right,' Melanie said. 'I'd better not.' Then, turning. 'Nick, I hope you're feeling better soon.'

'Thanks,' Nick muttered.

'Here, Melanie,' Dawn said. 'I'll see you to the door.'

They were only just out of the room before Christopher and Scott sniggered loudly.

'Shut it,' Nick said. 'Don't say a bloody word.'

'The state of it!' Scott said. 'Stick a mast through it and Ellen McArthur'd sail it round the world!'

'What worried me,' Christopher said, 'she'd said yes to Ben and Jerry's, none of us'd 've got a look in.'

'At least it wasn't her beat him up,' Scott said. 'Be in a worse state than he is now.'

They hadn't heard Dawn walking back into the room. 'You know,' she said into the midst of their laughter, 'I think it's time you grew up, the lot of you.' And she shut the bedroom door behind her hard.

It was a whole minute, maybe two, before any

of the boys touched their ice cream. 'I'm sorry,' Nick said.

Christopher and Scott were long gone and Nick had made his way, gingerly, to the toilet. His mother was in the living room watching some kind of quiz show while she applied varnish to her toes. Small puffs of cotton wool poked up from between each toe. The varnish was the colour of dark plums.

'No use saying you're sorry to me,' Dawn said.

Nick shrugged and hobbled a step away.

'While you're up,' Dawn said, 'why don't you try and have a proper wash? You must stink, laying round in that bed half the day.'

'It's not my fault.'

'I know.' Carefully, she ran the brush along the little toe of her right foot. 'Even so, you ought to do something. How about if I ran a bath? You could always sit on the edge.'

Nick shook his head. 'It's okay.'

'I could help with the bits you can't reach.'

'I don't think so.'

Dawn smiled. 'What? You don't think I haven't seen you . . .'

'Mum, just leave it, okay? Don't even go there.'

'All right. Suit yourself. Just offering to help.'

She went back to her toes and Nick shuffled slowly to the bathroom. Perhaps with some warm water and a flannel and a clean pair of boxers he'd smell less ripe.

★   ★   ★

80

A cushion at his back, Nick was able to sit at the table to eat. Chicken Rogon Josh, Lamb Passanda, Sag Aloo, pillaw rice and half a dozen papadums. Neither he nor his mother said very much until most of the food had gone.

'Lovely!' Dawn declared, pushing away her plate and reaching for a cigarette. 'But now I'm stuffed.'

'Do you have to?' Nick said, as Dawn's lighter flicked to life.

'It's just the one, Nick. Don't worry, one won't hurt.'

'It's not just one though, is it? It's one and one and . . .'

'Nick.'

'Okay, I'm sorry.'

'Here, have some of my beer.'

'Thanks.'

He drank and then released a low, slow burp.

'Charming!'

Nick broke off one of the last brittle edges of papadum and scraped up the residue of spicy sauce.

'Nick,' Dawn said abruptly. 'Just listen to me a minute.'

'No.'

'No what?'

'Just no.'

'No, you're not going to listen?'

'No, I'm not going to go to the police.'

They had been having this argument, back and forth, ever since Dawn had first spoken to him that morning.

'You ought to report what happened.'

'No.'

'It ought to be reported.'

'Why?'

'Why? A hundred reasons. Because it's a crime. Because if whoever did it isn't caught, the same thing could happen to somebody else. Because you could have lost an eye. Because you could have been killed.'

Nick looked at her evenly. 'Well, I wasn't, was I?'

'And that makes it all right? That makes it okay?'

'No, of course it doesn't. Don't be stupid.'

'I'm not being stupid. I want whoever did this to be put away.'

'Yeah, but they wouldn't be, would they? Slap on the wrist, community service, nothing. The same lot'd be back out, no time at all, and they'd know who'd grassed them up, turned them in.'

'And that's what you're afraid of?'

'No.'

'Is that what you're afraid of, whoever did this, they'd come after you again?'

'I'm not afraid, don't keep saying I'm afraid.'

'Then why . . .'

With a sweep of his arm, Nick sent empty food containers, glasses, plates and cutlery crashing to the floor.

'I am not afraid!' he shouted, and hobbled, as quickly as he was able, from the room.

★　★　★

His dad, Nick thought later, impossible to sleep. His father too frightened to step up on stage; the same person who years before had impressed his mum with his self-assurance, his lack of fear. How had that happened? Why had he changed?

Nick tugged at the quilt and rolled onto his side. Not me, he thought, that's not going to be me.

CHAPTER 12

The next few days passed more slowly than most. By the time he'd finally dragged himself out of bed his mother had been at work for hours and generally he saw no one until either Christopher or Scott or the pair of them came round after school. Lunch he fixed for himself in the microwave, heating up some frozen this or that. When he opened his art folder everything inside seemed pointless and boring. Whenever he tried settling down to read his book, he found concentration difficult. Five pages were sometimes all he could manage before his mind started wandering off and he'd realise that the last few sentences had meant nothing at all. And if he did get taken up by the story, rattling towards California with the Joad family in their '25 Dodge, either his stitches would start itching or a flash of pain, sharp and sudden, would shoot through him and break the thread.

Sometimes, when that happened, the pain, he closed his eyes and waited until it passed; sometimes, when it was especially severe, he went back to his room and lay on the bed. Dozing, drifting in and out of sleep, he would emerge again from the darkness of the tunnel and again the half-brick would hurtle through the light.

'What you gonna do about it?' Christopher had asked.

The same question he asked himself.

Confront Rawlings? Blevitt?

Do as his mum wanted, and hand it over to the police?

Have everyone know he'd had the crap beaten out of him and done nothing about it?

Just forget about it?

As if he could.

He slid his dad's tape into the stereo.

The mike so close he could hear the squeak of guitar strings as his father's fingers moved across the frets, pressing down.

The moment before he sings.

How long, how long has that evening train been gone?
How long? How long? Baby, how long?

From the box Nick took a ticket, torn and creased, for the Coliseum in St Martin's Lane, a Benefit Concert for Big Bill Broonzy, Sunday March 9th. £1. No mention of the year. Alongside that, folded once and once again, was a flier from the Hope & Anchor in Upper Street, the paper bleached white along the crease: Thurs., 11th, Jo

85

Ann Kelly; Mon., 15th, Les Harman; Tues., 16th, Dr Feelgood. And on a page from an old *Melody Maker*, in faint and faded print, there was an ad for the 100 Club in Oxford Street: Sunday, American Blues Legends, Sonny Terry and Brownie McGhee, and beneath, in smaller print, Les Harman and Charlie Bell.

The whistle blows, I can't see no train,
Deep down in my heart there's an aching pain.
How long, oh how long? Baby, how long?

Nick looked again at the pictures of his father and thought about the words he sang. Were they just words, songs he'd learned and liked to perform – they were, as far as Nick knew, other people's words after all – or were they more?

Feel so disgusted, empty too,
Don't know in this world, babe, what more
   I can do.
How long? How long? How long?

Nick thought he knew the answer. For his father the words had been true. Disgusted with himself and empty too. He had lived with it for so long and no longer. Until the moment he had first set foot on the ironwork of the bridge and begun to climb. The road below him, busy with cars. The wind, the words, cold and sharp in his ears. Don't know in this world what more I can do. How long,

86

Nick wondered, had he hesitated before he jumped? How long the fall?

Reaching out, Nick switched off the tape and realised someone was knocking at the front door.

It was Melanie, anxious and uncertain. Melanie, wearing a dress that hung shapelessly around her, some kind of cardigan around her shoulders, not quite covering her fleshy arms.

'I was wondering . . .' she began.

Nick looked at her and then looked at the floor.

'It's all right,' Melanie said, turning away. 'I'm sorry, it doesn't matter. I shouldn't have come.'

Nick shook his head. 'No, it's okay. Go on, what were you going to say?'

'I was wondering how you were, you know, feeling? How you were getting on?'

Nick shrugged. 'Okay. Not so bad, I suppose.' He couldn't quite bring himself to look her in the face.

Melanie stood there, wanting to say something more but unsure what.

'Look,' Nick said. 'The other day, when Chris and Scott were here, I'm sorry . . .'

'Oh, no. It's okay.'

'I never really said thank you properly.'

'There's no need.'

'The flowers . . .'

'It was nothing.'

'No, no. They were really nice. It was a nice thing to do.'

For a moment, Melanie's face relaxed into a smile.

'D'you want to come in or something?' Nick said.

'No, it's all right. I've got to . . .' She faltered, trying to think of something.

'Got to what?'

'Nothing.'

'So come in.'

As she walked hesitantly past him and into the kitchen, Nick wondered what on earth he was doing.

Melanie stopped by the kitchen table and glanced around.

'It's just like ours. Except for, you know, the stuff.'

'Yeah.'

'I suppose they all are.'

Nick nodded.

'Your mum at work?' Melanie said.

'Yeah.'

'Mine, too.'

'You're not at school?' Nick said.

Melanie shook her head. 'How long will you be off?' she asked.

'I dunno. Maybe next week. I've got to go back to the hospital first.'

'Have the stitches out.'

'Yes.'

'How many did you have?'

Nick touched them with his fingertips. 'Fifteen.'

He shifted his weight from one foot to the other.

'Do they hurt?'

'Not really, no. Itch sometimes.'

'I had stitches once. I was always pulling at them, 'cause of that, you know. Itching. I pulled some out before it was time. Didn't mean to. Blood everywhere. My mum, she went spare.'

As much for something to do as anything, Nick went to the side and picked up the kettle. 'Fancy a cup of tea?'

'No, it's all right.'

'Coffee, then?'

'No, I . . .'

'There might be a Coke still in the fridge.'

'I shouldn't.'

'Water? We do a very nice line in water.'

There was a vestige of a smile around Melanie's eyes. 'Tea, then. As long as you're making it, tea'd be fine.'

Nick filled the kettle and set it to boil.

'When I was waiting outside,' Melanie said. 'After I'd knocked the first time, I thought I heard someone singing.'

'Just an old tape,' Nick said, and then, because she continued to look at him. 'It was my dad.'

'Really?'

'Yeah.'

'Not really?'

'Yeah.'

'I didn't know your dad was a singer.'

'No, well, nor did I. I mean, I did, but not really. I'm just finding out.'

'Your dad's . . . your dad's dead, right?'

'Yes.'

'I wish mine was.'

The kettle started to boil.

Nick stared at her for several moments before speaking. 'You're not serious. I mean you're joking, right?'

Her look was unwavering, her eyes grey-green. 'Dead serious.'

Nick released a breath. 'How come?'

'The kettle's boiling,' Melanie said.

'How come you feel that way? About your dad?'

'The kettle,' Melanie said. She got up and moved towards it, banging her hip against the table corner on the way. 'Where's the tea?' she asked, a tremble in her voice.

Nick pointed to where the tea bags were on the shelf.

'What shall I make it in?' Melanie said.

Nick lifted down two mugs. Tears were running across the contours of Melanie's face. He dropped in the tea bags and she poured the water with a less than steady hand.

'He doesn't hit you, does he?' Nick asked. 'Or anything?'

He didn't want to go too far into what 'anything' might be.

'No,' Melanie said. 'He used to. Hit me, I mean. Now he won't . . . he won't even touch me. He just . . . he's just on at me all the time, calling me names. Fat bitch. Fat cow. Fat useless cunt.'

'I'm sorry,' Nick said and touched her arm.

Melanie sobbed and turned aside, her body starting to shake.

Nick swallowed hard, got the milk from the fridge and finished making the tea.

'Sugar?' he said.

She nodded and mumbled something he took to be 'Two.'

'Here,' he said a few moments later, holding the mug out towards her.

Melanie slowly turned and as she did so, she suddenly winced and doubled over as if she'd been kicked.

The mug shook in his hand and tea slopped to the floor.

'Here,' he said. 'Here, sit down.' But Melanie was shaking her head. 'The bathroom,' she said. 'I need to go to the bathroom.'

Nick nodded. 'You know where it is. Same as in your place, right?'

While she was gone he stood staring out of the window at the tops of cars moving fast between the lean branches of the trees. Buds slow to appear.

His mouth felt strangely dry, any discomfort of his own forgotten.

After a while, he heard the toilet flush, the bathroom door open and close.

'I'm sorry,' Melanie said.

'Don't be silly,' Nick said.

Melanie gave him a smile and reached for her tea.

'That'll be cold,' Nick said.

'Doesn't matter.'

'I don't know if there's any biscuits,' Nick said.

Melanie sat on one of the stools. 'Tell me about your dad,' she said. 'If you want to, that is.'

Before Nick could respond there was a knock at the door.

'I don't believe it,' he said. 'Oxford Circus round here all of a sudden.'

When he opened the door there was Ellen, snug black top, black jeans, her hair teased out.

'Oh,' Nick said.

Behind him, Ellen could see through the small hall and into the kitchen, Melanie sitting there, mug of tea cradled in both hands.

'Sorry,' Ellen said. 'I didn't want to disturb anything.'

'What? No, no. It's nothing. Come in.'

Ellen looked at him with narrowed eyes. 'I don't think so, Nick, do you?' And before he could stop her, she had closed the door. When he pulled it back open it was only to hear her feet, fast on the stairs.

'Shit!' he said, not quite to himself. 'Bloody shit!' And turned back to where Melanie was now standing, face doughy and pale. Distraught.

'I'll go,' she said.

Nick nodded and looked away.

CHAPTER 13

The pub was almost empty when Nick walked in. A couple of blokes sitting at a table to the far right, nursing their pints. Someone in a suit close by the window, newspaper folded open in front of him, occasionally looking out. Stripped wooden tables and a bare wood floor. A shamrock over the bar.

He waited, patient, as the barman shelved a case of Becks with unwonted care.

When the man straightened and turned, he looked at the stitches neat along Nick's forehead but made no remark.

'There used to be some kind of acoustic club upstairs,' Nick said. 'Folk and blues. I don't think it happens any more.'

'You're right there.'

'Whoever used to run it, you've no idea how I might get hold of them?'

The barman leaned closer. 'A singer, then, is that what you are? Not country and western, I dare say?' Throwing his head back, he sang the opening lines of 'Blue Moon of Kentucky' in a strangled tone. 'Bill Monroe, now, there's your man.'

94

'Have you any idea,' Nick said, 'who it was, ran the club? How I might get in touch?'

'Dave Brunner,' the barman said, aiming his voice at the two men in the corner, 'have either of you seen him around at all?'

'Didn't he used to use the Grenadier?' one said.

'I believe you're right,' said the other.

'The Grenadier,' Nick said. 'Where's that?'

'Gaisford Street,' said the first man. 'Last time I looked.'

'Dave Brunner,' Nick said to the barman. 'That's his name?'

'The same.'

'Thanks,' Nick said and turned towards the door.

'*Blue Moon of Kentucky, keep on shining,*' warbled the barman. '*Shine on the one who's gone and said goodbye.*'

Kentish Town Road was the usual mixture of slow-moving traffic and impatient pedestrians, beggars sitting hopefully alongside cash machines, young women pushing buggies and prams. Nick had taken a couple of painkillers earlier but still walked slowly, short of breath, not wanting to jar his ribs any more than was necessary. He was crossing the junction with Holmes Road when he heard someone call his name.

'Nick? Nick Harman, isn't it?'

She was standing back from the pavement edge,

neatly dressed, hair in place, leather brief case in her hand.

'Detective Inspector Ferris, remember?'

Of course he remembered. He wanted to brush past, carry on walking, but didn't quite feel able.

'No school?'

Nick shook his head.

She was looking at the stitches etched across his forehead.

'You come off your bike, something like that?'

'Yeah.'

'What? You came off your bike, that's how it happened?'

'If you say so.'

'If I say so?'

'Look,' Nick said, taking a step round her. 'I've got to go.'

'You're not in any kind of trouble, Nick, are you?'

'Why should I be in trouble?'

'You tell me.'

An ambulance, siren wailing, was trying to force it's way through the middle of the traffic, cars and lorries pulling over to let it pass. People bunched on the corner where they were standing, scarcely bothering to look.

'That's a nasty cut,' the inspector said.

Nick shrugged, not answering.

'How many stitches, Nick?'

Nick shrugged again.

'You weren't in some kind of a fight, were you?'

'I told you, I came off my bike.'

'Of course.' The inspector smiled. 'Do you even have a bike?'

'All kids have bikes, don't they?'

She raised a hand towards his face. 'Whoever did that, I don't suppose you'd care to tell me who it was?'

'I've got to go.'

'You don't always have to fight your own battles, Nick, fight your own corner.'

'No?'

The inspector shook her head. 'Not on your own. Sometimes it's okay to ask for help.'

'I don't need any help.'

He had half an idea she might try to stop him, but when he glanced back at the next crossing, she was no longer there. As he reached the far side of the road, someone hurrying cannoned into him, and he gasped and caught his breath as the pain fired across his chest, leaning for several moments against a shop window before continuing.

The Grenadier was at the far end of Gaisford Street, a small, low pub he'd never noticed before, squeezed between a builder's yard and a terrace of ageing flat-fronted houses late-flowering with skips and scaffolding.

It took him less than a few minutes to learn this was indeed Dave Brunner's local and that

Brunner showed up most nights a little after ten, having switched off his set at the start of the news.

By the time Nick had walked back home, he was aching so much he swallowed two Paracetamol with a glass of water and lay on the bed.

The first time Nick had seen Christopher's house he'd been eaten up with envy. All of his life in one cramped flat or another and here was Christopher with more rooms than you could easily count. And stairs. More than anything, Nick was jealous of the stairs. However old he was then – eleven, twelve – the idea of stairs, stairs you could chase up and down, even lay practically full-length along, was somehow thrilling.

And at the top of the stairs, in a loft space let into the attic and going right across the house, was Christopher's room, shelves and cupboards overflowing with books and toys, a remote control train set in one corner, his own stereo, his own computer, his own small TV.

The first time Nick had been allowed to sleep over, he swore he would never go home again.

Of course, after that, as he got older, it became clear that all was not as perfect as it seemed. Voices raised in anger, slamming doors. Sometimes Christopher would sit cross-legged on his bed for hours, still wearing his outdoor clothes, hands clamped over his ears.

When Nick came round one day in the summer holidays, there was a van outside, two men loading boxes and small items of furniture, clothes wrapped in plastic. Christopher's younger sister, Kirsten, sat on the step outside crying. His mother, grim-faced, directed operations, anxious to leave, her new Range Rover parked a short distance up the hill.

They had been in Oxford less than a month, Christopher's mother and sister, when Christopher's old baby sitter, Anna, a Bulgarian blonde with a student visa, moved in. It was longer than that before Christopher would as much as speak to her, never mind use her name. He still referred to her dismissively as 'the baby-sitter', though that didn't stop him watching hopefully as she padded to the bathroom in the mornings, her dressing gown loose but never quite loose enough.

This particular evening, Christopher's dad was out at the theatre and Anna was stretched out on the settee with a bottle of wine, watching a DVD of *Indecent Proposal*.

'Tell me again why we're going to this pub?' Christopher asked.

Hungry, he was making a search of the fridge, one of those huge American jobs with metallic fronts and half the contents of Waitrose inside.

'See this bloke,' Nick said.

'About this woman, used to sing with your old man.'

'Yeah.'

99

Christopher finished making a sandwich with ham and cheese, cut it across and offered half to Nick, who shook his head.

'Come on,' Christopher said, 'if we're going, let's go. I can eat this on the way.'

The interior of the pub was a broad L-shape, with two pool tables at the far end. A few heads turned towards Nick and Christopher as they entered, but mostly they were paid scant attention. The woman behind the bar, middle-aged, served them two bottles of Carlsberg without question. There was a television fixed by an angle bracket to the wall, the sound turned low, and through speakers high on the far side of the room, just audible, slow deep soul.

'James Carr,' said Christopher, who liked to know such things. '"Dark End of the Street". My old man's got the album.'

Nick nodded and took a swig at his beer. Christopher's dad had enough old vinyl to start a retro store.

'Excuse me,' he said to the woman behind the bar, 'but can you tell us if Dave Brunner's here?'

'Dave? Yes, see that bloke over there, bald, glasses. That's Dave.'

Nick thanked her and nudged Christopher's arm. Together they walked over to where Brunner was talking to a couple who might have been father and son, the conversation, what they picked up, about how Spurs had thrown it away again in the last ten minutes. Nick was surprised they'd held out that long. A quick image of Ellen slipped into his mind and was as quickly gone.

'Mr Brunner,' he said. 'Sorry to interrupt you . . .'

Brunner turned his head. 'Good news or bad?'

'Neither really.'

'Then you must be collecting for something.'

Nick shook his head. 'I just wanted to ask you . . .'

'Yes?'

'You used to run that club, right? In the high street?'

'Spit it out, son.'

'Charlene Bell . . .'

'What about her?'

'I was wondering, if you knew how I could get it touch with her?'

Dave Brunner chuckled. 'Bit old for you, son,' he said, winking at the couple across the table.

Tosser, Nick thought. 'She was a friend of my dad's.'

'And he's sent you to look for her, has he? What's he think I am, Friends bloody Reunited?'

'My dad's dead,' Nick said.

The grin disappeared from Brunner's face. 'I'm sorry,' he said, and then, 'What was his name?'

'Les Harman.'

Brunner leaned back and looked at Nick as if for the first time. 'Sit down,' he said. 'The pair of you. Let me get you another beer.'

CHAPTER 14

Charlene Bell lived in a large four-storey house in Camberwell, south London. Miles. Euston, Kingsway, Waterloo, the Elephant: Nick thought the bus was never going to arrive.

The house was at the middle of a terrace that had formed one side of a Georgian square, now partly demolished, largely in need of repair. Charlene had bought it with the proceeds of a freak hit some dozen years before; a television commercial had used an old recording she'd made of 'Walking the Dog' and for a couple of weeks it had hovered in the lower reaches of the Top Twenty.

Her record company, having ignored her for years, hastily reissued the album from which the song came and of course nobody bought it. Charlene appeared on daytime TV and Greater London Radio, as it was then, chatting with Robert Elms. Bizarrely, she was added to an Oldies tour which featured the Tremeloes, Billie Davis and the Four Pennies. Aberystwyth, Truro, Derby Assembly Rooms.

Then it was all over. Charlene went back to doing the occasional gig in clubs where sixty people exceeded the fire regulations. Her sudden windfall she invested in the house, which she did up and rented out, room by room, living herself in the raised ground floor flat where Nick found her, Saturday morning, just a few days after Dave Brunner had given him her number and Nick had phoned, asking if it would be all right to come round.

Charlene met him at the front door. She was tall, taller than he'd expected from the photograph, wearing a long, loose dress in shades of green. Her hair was still thick and curly, but some of the curls had turned to grey.

'So you're Les's boy,' she said. 'You're Nick.' And embarrassed him with a quick hug. When she released him and stepped back there was a suggestion of tears at the corners of her eyes.

'Come in,' she said. 'Come on in. I've been down the baker's. Fresh croissants. Amazing what you can get in Camberwell these days.'

The room into which she led him was crowded with furniture – two settees and several chairs – framed photographs, books and magazines. A piano near the window. Faded patterned rugs on polished boards. Flowers in odd-shaped jugs and vases. A small round table with pale blue mugs, white plates, a coffee pot, jam.

'These are just nicely warm,' Charlene said,

bringing in the promised croissants. 'Take a seat. Dig in.'

Nick looked around: cats lay curled amongst the cushions that were scattered liberally across both settees.

'Just shoo them off, they won't bite. Except Bessie there . . .' She indicated a chocolate brown Burmese that was staring at Nick with violet eyes. 'She'd take a piece out of you without thinking twice. And you look as if you've been in the wars enough already.'

Self-consciously, Nick touched the stitches on his forehead.

While he still hesitated, Charlene picked up a pair of tabbies, one in each hand – 'Mamie, Clara, come on now.' – and deposited them, complaining loudly, on the ground.

'There.'

Nick perched on one end of the settee and when Charlene sat opposite, a cat, one he hadn't seen before, immediately jumped into her lap.

The coffee was strong, stronger than he was used to, and the croissant crumbled into fragments in his hand.

'Don't worry,' Charlene said. 'The cats will hoover it up later.' She reached down and set her mug on the floor. 'So,' she said, smiling, 'you want to know about your dad?'

'Yes, I suppose.'

'You're not sure?'

'No. I mean, yes. Yes, I am.'

'Your mum – Dawn, isn't it?' Nick nodded. 'She doesn't talk about him?'

'Not really, no.'

'She's got her reasons, I dare say.'

'What do you mean?'

'Well, doing what he did. Leaving her with you when you were what? Six? Seven?'

'Seven.'

'I doubt he left any money. Debts, more like. It can't have been easy.'

Nick shrugged. He didn't know, though he supposed it was true. He'd never gone hungry, he knew that. He knew his mum worked all the hours going, still did.

'He was a stubborn bugger, Les. Get an idea stuck in his head and that was it. Music especially.' Charlene smiled, remembering. 'Sixties, for instance, everyone was going electric. All the blues bands. Guitar solos fit to pierce your ear drums. Saxophones. John Mayall. Fleetwood Mac.' Charlene shook her head. 'I was in this pub once with your dad, Bromley of all places. And this producer, promoter, whatever – Mike Vernon, I think it was, could have been – going on and on at your dad, wanting him to put a band together, go out on the road, get into the studio, record. He could've done it, too, Les, he had the talent and, God knows, the charm. When he wanted. Charm the birds down from the proverbial trees when he'd a mind. Audiences liked him. He could've jumped on the bandwagon, changed his style. Grabbed some money while it was there.'

'So why didn't he?'

Charlene reached for her coffee. 'Selling out, that's what he called it. He'd had the chance before, when he first started. Talent scouts sniffing round the Two I's, skiffle, rock "n" roll. He was nice-looking, too, when he was young, your dad, that would have helped. But no, he wasn't going to be another Cliff Richard, Adam Faith. Not even Lonnie Donegan. What he cared about was the music, keeping it pure.'

'You worked with him, though.'

''Course I did. He was lovely. A lovely player. You'd sing and he'd listen. Play what was right. Never try and upstage you, like some. And when he sang himself – he never had the strongest voice, he'd've been the first to admit – but the way it came out. Like, you know, he meant every word.'

She drank her coffee till it was gone, reached for the pot and poured some more.

'He was happy enough working with me, at least I think he was. A few others, maybe. But up there by himself with a guitar, singing blues, that's what he liked most. That's when he was really himself. Whereas me . . .' Charlene laughed. '. . . I was a real whore where music's concerned, still am if I get the chance. Northern Soul weekends at Pontins, tribute bands, jazz. Rhythm and Blues Revival Festival a couple of months from now. Whitby Pavilion.' She laughed again. 'Long as I can get there cheap with my bus pass and a senior railcard, I'll give it a go.'

Charlene – 'Call me Charlie, for heaven's sake. Everyone else does.' – gave him the grand tour of her museum of photographs, mostly shots of her with musicians or singers Nick failed to recognise and whose names meant little or nothing. Only Eric Clapton, on stage at a benefit concert for somebody or other, gave him pause for thought – Charlene herself centre right, face half obscured by some bloke with long frizzy hair she assured him used to play for Led Zeppelin.

And, of course, there were pictures of her with his dad, half a dozen in all, different places, different times.

'Come in here,' Charlene said. 'I want to show you this.'

Here was her music room, complete with keyboard and miniature mixing desk, speakers, mikes and numerous guitars. One of these she reached down and put into Nick's hands.

'I won't lie to you, this was never your dad's first choice. Nor second, either. But it was his, he played it. In fact if you look back at his photos next door, the one taken at the Marquee, this is what he's playing there.'

Nick looked down at the instrument, the smooth grain of the wood, reddish-blonde, the dust that had collected along one edge and between the strings.

'I don't suppose you play?'

Nick shook his head.

'Well, take it anyway. A souvenir. Les'd be glad for you to have it, I'm sure. And who knows? One day you might learn. I'll teach you if you like.'

'I don't think so.'

'Suit yourself.'

There were a hundred more questions he was sure he wanted to ask but none would come to mind. When he left Charlene kissed him impulsively on the cheek.

'Come back and see me. Any time.'

When he walked back into the flat, a good hour later, carrying the guitar in its cracked leather case, his mother turned away and hid her face in her hands.

CHAPTER 15

Monday, Nick went back down Kentish Town with his camera and a new roll of film, but through the viewfinder everything looked dull and uninspiring. The same as before. When he tried to take a picture of a shaggy-haired man squatting on a blanket outside the Halifax, the man swore at him angrily and the dog tried to take a bite out of his leg. So much for becoming the new Dorothea Lange.

He sort of wished he'd gone back to school, except he wanted to wait until his stitches came out and that would be another four days.

His mum had left him a few quid to get something for lunch and he pocketed it and had a couple of bowls of cereal instead, corn flakes mixed with Cheerios.

There was an old film on afternoon TV, something about a boxer who was supposed to take a fall but changed his mind and knocked his opponent all over the ring. He paid for it in the end.

Nick looked at his watch and decided to get changed. He had a plan. He'd seen Ellen cutting through the estate from time to time on her way home, and although he couldn't be certain she'd be there today, he thought he might as well give it a try.

Twenty minutes later he was ready. Boots and jeans didn't give him a lot of choice, but there was a grey t-shirt without too many creases he found near the bottom of the drawer and over that he was wearing a near-black Adidas top with white stripes running parallel along the sleeves. A month or so ago he'd borrowed it from Christopher and forgotten to give it back.

In the bathroom, he tried gelling his hair and hated the result, but by then it was too late.

Sod it!

His timing, though, was spot on. Passing between two sets of garages, he stepped out into a small courtyard between tower blocks and there was Ellen, art folder under one arm, walking briskly towards the far corner. Trainers, black with a red stripe and double velcro straps, long denim skirt; a pink scarf hung loose over her shoulders and her black beret was angled back on her head.

'Hi!' Nick said, feigning surprise.

'Hello.' Ellen walked on a few paces and then stopped. 'What are you doing here?'

Nick shrugged. 'Nothing special.'

'Just hanging out.'

'Yeah.'

'You wouldn't've been waiting here for me, would you?' Ellen said.

111

'No way.'

'You sure?'

'Course I'm sure.'

'That's all right, then.'

She was looking straight at him, amusement in her eyes. Nick stared at the ground then looked away. He knew what he'd intended to say, but what had sounded fine inside his head now didn't feel right.

'How's the project going?' Ellen said finally. 'The photography.'

'Okay, I suppose. Yeah.'

Ellen nodded.

'You?'

'Oh, you know.'

'Yeah.'

A plane went over, lower than usual, banking through cloud.

'Maybe I could look at it sometime?' Nick said. 'Your folder, you know.'

'It's in a mess at the moment. I mean, there's nothing . . .'

'No, no, that's okay. I just . . .'

'Yes.' Ellen took a breath. 'I'm sorry about what happened, your head and everything. Laura told me you got beaten up pretty bad.'

'Yeah, well . . .'

'You'll have a scar.'

'Prob'ly.'

She was looking at him now as though a scar might not be such a bad thing.

'The other day,' Nick said, 'when you came round . . .'

'I didn't mean to interrupt.'

'You didn't.'

'You and your girl friend.'

'Come on, she's not . . .'

'What?'

'Me and Melanie . . . You don't think . . .'

'I don't see why not.'

'Gross!'

'Well, if you don't fancy her, someone obviously somebody did.'

'What d'you mean?'

'She's pregnant, isn't she?'

'No, she's not, she's just fat.'

Ellen raised an eyebrow. 'Ask her then, why don't you? Next time she calls round.'

And with that she walked away, leaving Nick feeling perplexed and not a little stupid. Melanie pregnant, up the stick, in the family way. The thought of it made him slightly sick.

A couple of kids Nick vaguely recognised from lower down the school were skulking beneath a walkway, smoking. Four or five skateboarders trying to find new ways of breaking their legs. A boy in an Arsenal shirt, Pires lettered across the back, practising wheelies. When Nick turned the corner, some forty metres from his own block, there was Ross Blevitt, leaning back against the pebbled wall, half a dozen others gathered round him.

113

Nick hesitated, then carried on.

Blevitt said something to his crew and slowly they moved away. Not far.

As Nick drew almost level, Blevitt eased himself from the wall.

'So, Nicky . . .'

'Nick.'

'Whatever.'

Blevitt raised a hand towards Nick's forehead and Nick knocked it away.

'Ain't so good at takin' warnings,' Blevitt said.

Nick waited.

'Cosyin' up to the police. Givin' 'em names.'

'Bollocks.'

'Seen you, man. Down the town. You and that bitch. Detective inspector, i'n' it?'

'She's the one, started talking to me. What was I supposed to do?'

'Walk away. Keep your mouth closed.'

Nick said nothing.

'I'm tellin' you, man.'

'Yeah? What's it gonna be? Another brick when I'm not looking?'

Blevitt jabbed a finger against Nick's chest. 'Keep talkin' to the wrong people, you're gonna find out, right? A few stitches. Couple broken ribs. That's nothin'.'

Nick held Blevitt's stare, then walked round him.

He carried on walking and at the last moment Blevitt's crew grudgingly stepped back, allowing him just enough room to get past.

He heard one of them hawking phlegm into his throat and felt spittle in his hair and on his neck. Nick clenched his fists and kept on going, damned if he was going to give them the satisfaction of watching him wipe it away.

CHAPTER 16

Steve Rawlings had been watching the encounter between Blevitt and Nick from the eighth floor balcony. Waiting for the moment when Blevitt would take him apart. But instead, Blevitt had simply stood there and let him walk away.

Rawlings spat at the ground.

First Harman had dissed him in front of his mates and then, more than likely, grassed him up to the police.

Next time he wouldn't get off so easy.

Next time it'd be more than just a beating.

'What d'you reckon, Steve?' asked one of the boys alongside him.

Rawlings spat again. 'I reckon someone's gonna teach Harman a real lesson.'

'Ross didn't do nothin' 'cept mouth off at him.'

'Ross's a pussy,' Rawlings said, lowering his voice to ensure Blevitt, still standing below, didn't hear him.

'You gonna take him?'

'Yeah, when I'm ready.'

For reassurance, Rawlings touched the Stanley knife, hard and cool in the pocket of his Diesel jeans.

'Oh, man,' Scott said with a shake of his head, 'that's so not cool.'

They were in Nick's room, Scott and Nick on the bed, Christopher sitting on the floor, head resting back against the wall. One of Scott's old Aphex Twin CDs was on the stereo.

'You were the one, telling me I should do something,' Nick said. 'Make a move.'

'Yeah, but not like that.'

'Why not?'

'It's too obvious, right? There's Ellen on her way home and you just happen to be there, standing round with a hard-on and your tongue hanging out. Pathetic.'

'My tongue wasn't hanging out.'

'You just had a hard-on.'

Nick aimed a punch at Scott's shoulder and, laughing, he sprawled out of reach.

'You do fancy her, though?' Christopher said. 'Can we establish that as a matter of record?'

'She's okay, yeah.'

'You fancy her?'

'Yeah, if you like.'

'If *I* like?'

'All Chris fancies,' Scott said, 'is the baby-sitter.'

'She's not the baby-sitter.'

'Okay, then. Stepmother.'

'And she's not my bloody stepmother.'

'What is she then?'

'Nothing,' Christopher said, just this side of flustered. 'What are we talking about her for anyway? It's Ellen we're meant to be discussing, Nick and Ellen.'

'Laura reckons she's hot,' Scott said.

'How does she know?'

'She was going out with this bloke, last term. Black guy. Twenty-three, twenty-four.'

'You're kidding.'

'Straight up.'

'Who was he?'

'DJ.'

'Where from?'

'Brixton. Notting Hill. All over.'

'She's not seeing him any more?'

'Laura says no.'

'There you go, Nick, she's yours.'

'Already popped her cork.'

'Shut it,' Nick said.

'Bloke like that, only way he's gonna . . .'

'I said shut it, right?'

'Okay, okay, she's still a virgin, that's what you want to believe. *Virgo intacta.*'

Nick hit him on the arm, just below the elbow, and the impact jarred back along his own arm and into his chest, making him wince with pain.

'You okay?' Christopher asked, concerned.

'Never mind him,' Scott said, 'what about me?'

'What about you?'

'I'm the one got hit.'

'No more'n you deserved.'

'Thanks a lot.'

Aphex Twin had come to an end and Christopher was rummaging through Nick's meagre collection of CDs.

Scott tapped out a cigarette. 'Anyone got a light?'

'Not in here,' Nick said.

'Oh, come on . . .'

'Not in here.'

'Suppose I roll a joint?'

'That's different.'

'Great thinking,' Christopher said, 'protect your lungs and scramble your brain.'

''S'not exactly LSD,' Scott said. 'Besides, you gonna say no to a drag?'

'No way.'

Scott laughed, reaching for his papers.

'Anyway,' Christopher continued, 'it's medicinal, right? Good for the pain in Nick's ribs, got to be.'

While Scott was skinning up, the door bell rang.

'Not your mum, is it?' Christopher asked. 'Forgot her keys.'

'Shouldn't think so.'

The bell rang again.

'Maybe it's Ellen,' Scott said.

It was Melanie. Distressed, lumpen, her eyes red from crying.

Oh, Christ, Nick thought. He didn't say anything.

'I just . . .' Melanie began. 'I . . . I don't know, I shouldn't've come, I just . . . just wanted someone to talk to, I . . .'

Her words faltered to a halt.

Look at her, Nick thought, she's in a real state. What harm can it do? Ask her in. 'I'm sorry,' he said. 'It's not a good time. I've got mates round. I . . .'

'It's all right,' Melanie said. 'Mates. I understand.'

Releasing him, she looked away.

Nick hesitated, no more than a moment, and closed the door.

'You're gonna have to cut that out,' Scott said, 'Having her sneak down like that.'

'Melanie doesn't sneak anywhere,' Christopher said.

'I'm serious,' Scott said. 'She's almost screwed it up for you and Ellen once already. And that's before you've even got started.' Fishing around in one of the kitchen drawers, he found a box of matches. 'Unless you really do fancy her, of course.'

'You looking to get thumped again?' Nick said.

'I saw this programme,' Christopher said, 'the other night. About blokes who fancy really fat women.'

'Thanks, Christopher,' Nick said.

'I'm talking seriously fat, yeah? Twenty, thirty stone.'

'Gross me out,' Scott said, pointing two fingers down his throat.

'And there's these blokes, right, called feeders. Once they've got into a relationship with one of these women, they keep making them eat more and more, fattening them up.'

'What the hell for?'

'I dunno. I fell asleep.'

'Least we know what Melanie was after,' Scott said. 'Nick was late with her after-dinner snack. Fries, burgers and a tub of ice cream.'

'Elephant flavour,' Christopher suggested.

'Chocolate sauce,' Nick said.

'Hundreds and thousands.'

'Ketchup.'

'Tomato sauce.'

Nick reached for the joint. 'You think it could be true?' he said. 'Melanie being pregnant?'

'Who knows?' Christopher said.

'Who cares?' said Scott.

Nick took another hit. When he closed his eyes he could still see Melanie's face as she turned away, swollen and sore.

'You sure about this, Steve?'

'Just keep your eyes open and your mouth shut.'

'Doin' it ourselves, I mean.'

'What you scared of?'

'I'm not scared.'

'Then shut up.'

'I just thought we should tell, Ross, that's all.'

'What'cha wanna tell Ross for?'

'You know.'

'No, I don't know. Now shut it.'

They were shadowed by the overhang of the railway arch, Steve Rawlings and the three that hung with him most: Josh, Casper and Harry. Cans of cheap lager and the glow of cigarettes in the dark. Rawlings feeling sharp in his new D & G Basics top, the one with the blue and green stripes around the neck, the green stripe on the sleeve.

Not so many people used the cut-through now, not after the hoo-hah about muggings in the local press, but there were still a few. Suits late back from the City, men who'd stopped off for a drink or two or spent an hour in the gym, working out. Women too.

'Here,' Casper hissed. 'How 'bout this one now?'

The click of heels fast along the paving slabs. Someone hurrying home after a busy day, looking forward to a gin and tonic and a warm bath.

'Yeah,' Rawlings said. 'Tasty. She'll do.'

He waited until she was almost level before stepping clear.

'Excuse me, miss.'

The woman gasped, startled. Brown hair,

expensively cut; pale grey suit, leather bag over one shoulder, laptop in its case in her left hand.

'Sorry, didn't mean to frighten you.'

'No, it's not that.'

'You haven't got a light?'

'Yes, I think so . . .'

Hearing a movement behind her, she turned, and darting forward Josh seized the strap of her shoulder bag and pulled it from her arm; a moment later, Harry barged into her back and Casper grabbed the laptop and wrenched it free.

Still in front of her, Rawlings reached towards the gold chain at her neck and she seized his arm with both hands.

'Leggo, you stupid bitch!'

Digging her nails into the flesh of his arm, bare above the wrist, she kicked him hard in the shins.

'Steve! Come on, come on!'

While Steve hesitated, Josh and Casper had already broken into a run.

The woman started to scream and the knife came out of Rawlings' pocket as if with a will of its own, thumb flicking the blade free as it swung past her face and sank into her arm. As the metal sliced through wool and silk and skin the scream changed pitch, accelerating with fear and pain.

Rawlings tore himself away, pushing her as she stumbled back, fingers fastening round the chain and pulling it hard enough to break the clasp.

'Bitch!' he said once more and spat down into her face, before legging it away. Stupid bitch, grabbing at him like that, serve her right.

CHAPTER 17

Jackie Ferris had been anticipating a relatively easy day: a meeting with representatives of the local traders' group at ten, lunch with an old colleague who'd retired to the Isle of Wight, a session with the planning committee at three. Relax and leave the hard policing to the troops.

No way.

Before nine she was standing in the superintendent's office, smarting as he outlined the extent of her inadequacies. Arrest rates were a joke. Home Office targets relating to street crime were in jeopardy. There was talk about no-go areas in the press and on the local news. Public confidence was in danger of being irrevocably lost.

The superintendent's tirade was a colourful mixture of foul language and management jargon which left little room for doubt: if things didn't improve and fast, if arrests weren't made and the current spate of robberies stopped – if, in short, the detective inspector and her team didn't get some results and fast – she would spend the rest of her career sharpening pencils and helping old biddies across the road.

'Am I clear?'

'Yes, sir.'

'Because I've already had the Deputy Assistant Commissioner on the phone this morning, offering to hang my balls out to dry.'

'I'm sorry, sir.'

'And before that happens to me, I'll make good and sure something similar happens to you, by means of whatever appendage is convenient. Understood?'

'Yes, sir.'

'Right. Now get out of here and get it sorted.'

The name of the woman who had been attacked and robbed was Victoria Coleman. Despite her injuries, she had managed to get back on to the main road and wave down a passing car; the driver had called 999 on his mobile and instead of driving her to Accident and Emergency himself, he'd elected to wait with her for the ambulance. Possibly he was worried about the blood on his upholstery.

At the Royal Free, she'd been treated for wounds and shock and kept in overnight. Jackie Ferris's first priority was to check how the incident had been dealt with.

The control room – computer-aided-despatch room, to give it it's proper title – was on the first floor and when Ferris entered there were three civilian staff, headsets in place, busily answering calls while Magic 105.4 played gently in the background.

A man was prancing naked around the tennis courts on Parliament Hill Fields and refusing either to cover up or leave; a shoplifter had been detained in Sommerfield's, two bunches of bananas, one free-range chicken and a large mango and vanilla organic yoghurt about her person – obviously a shoplifter concerned with her bodily well-being – and a lorry-mounted crane had been in collision with an ambulance at the corner of York Rise and Chetwynd Road, blocking traffic in all four directions.

'E, S and I,' announced Jeff Parks, the officer in charge. 'In that order.'

Ferris knew these were ways of prioritising calls. I stood for Immediate, S for Soon and E for Extended. An I-grade call should be dealt with inside twelve minutes, an S grade in an hour. At that rate the man on the tennis courts would be entertaining pre-school kids and their au-pairs for some time to come.

'Jackie,' Jeff Parks said. 'How's it going?'

When she had transferred to the station as a uniform sergeant some years before, Parks had been her supervising officer. Now, with a gammy leg and a photograph of his first grandchild in his back pocket, he ran the control room.

'Been better,' Ferris said.

'Last night? Aggravated burglary?'

'Yes.'

Parks brought up the information on his computer.

'Call came in at 21.17, designated Immediate. It was assigned five minutes later, PCs Lamont and Handley, they'd been dealing with a disturbance at Prince of Wales Road, outside Pizza Express. Arrived at the scene 21.26. Approximately five minutes ahead of the ambulance.' Parks smiled. 'Well inside the target.'

Ferris nodded. Three minutes inside. 'Okay, Jeff,' she said. 'Thanks, keep up the good work.'

As she left the radio was playing Joan Armatrading: 'Love and Affection'.

Adam Lamont was young, keen, armed with a degree in Social Politics from London Metropolitan University; Diane Handley was older and more streetwise, for all that she had left school at sixteen with three grade Cs and a D. Which one, Jackie Ferris wondered, was going to make it up the ladder first? She caught up with them in the canteen, about to begin their first shift.

'Tea, ma'am?' Lamont asked, half out of his seat as he saw her approach. 'Coffee?'

'Neither, thanks.'

Lamont sat back down.

'Last night,' Ferris said, 'Victoria Coleman, you took the call.'

'Yes, ma'am,' Lamont said. 'Laptop stolen, credit cards, mobile phone, close to a hundred and twenty pounds in cash – she'd stopped off at the cash point on her way from the station – and a gold chain from round her neck.'

'She had a nasty cut on her arm,' Handley said. 'Obviously pretty shaken up.'

'You got a chance to talk to her?'

'I rode with her in the ambulance,' Handley said. 'Thought it might be a good time. She says there were three attacked her for certain, maybe four. She thinks they'd been hiding under the railway bridge, waiting. One of them stopped her to ask for a light and the others jumped her from behind.'

'What on earth was she doing walking that way alone anyway?'

'Short cut home, ma'am. Maisonette on Croftdown Road.'

Jackie Ferris shook her head. 'Descriptions?'

'The one who spoke to her, yes. Young, she says. Fifteen, sixteen. Five-seven or eight. Jeans, lightish coloured long-sleeved top. Woollen hat on his head, dark, pulled down towards his eyes.'

'Race?'

'White.'

'Could be half a hundred kids. Anything on the others?'

'Not really, no. She didn't get a good look at any of them.'

'But the one she saw, he was the one that stabbed her?'

'Yes.'

'After the ambulance had left, I searched the immediate area,' Lamont said. 'No sign of a weapon.'

'Okay. Good work,' Ferris said. She was back

on her feet. She needed to get her team out and about, asking questions, calling in favours, knocking on doors. And she had to call the hospital and find out if Victoria Coleman had been released.

The first thing Jackie Ferris noticed, almost everything in the room was grey or white – the covers on the chairs, the rug, the paint upon the walls. Victoria Coleman had only let the inspector in after scrutinizing her warrant card through the fish eye peephole in the door. Her skin seemed unnaturally pale and her right arm was in a sling.

'If you want coffee,' she said, 'you'd best give me a hand. Otherwise it's likely to end up on the floor.'

They sat in the bay-fronted window, trees in leaf in the street outside.

'I hope you haven't come to tell me how stupid I was.'

Ferris shook her head.

'You never think it's going to happen to you.'

The inspector didn't know if that were true. Lots of people, older ones especially, were too frightened to venture out after six at night. Victoria Coleman wasn't one of those. She was young, bright, well-dressed and well-paid and worked out in the gym three times a week.

'My friends tell me, carry an alarm, get some – what is it? – mace.'

'Do you think they would have helped?'

'Probably not.'

'I know you gave a description to the officers at the scene, I wonder if you'd mind going through it again?'

The inspector listened carefully but learned nothing new. 'The youth who attacked you, do you think you'd recognise him again?'

The reply was slow in coming. 'I want to say yes, of course I do. I lay half the night in that hospital bed, trying to picture him in my mind. You know, get it clear. Exactly what he looked like. But, in truth, I'm not sure I can.' She lowered her eyes. 'I'm sorry.'

'That's okay,' Jackie Ferris said, disappointed.

'There is one thing . . .'

'Yes.'

'Before they ran off, I think one of them used a name. Steve. Steve, come on, that's what he said.'

CHAPTER 18

Nick took the guitar out of its case and sat on the edge of the bed, the instrument resting on his knee. Left hand holding the neck, he pressed the thumb of his right hand uncertainly against the top string. Pulled and released, the sound flat and unsatisfying. He tried again, the first then all the other strings, six in all. Bass to treble, low to high. Slow then fast, fast and then slow. When he tried simultaneously pressing his fingertips down on the strings higher up, it altered the sound, not necessarily for the better.

Truth was, he didn't have a clue what he was doing, not a clue.

'Hey, Django,' came his mother's voice from the hall, 'how about some breakfast?'

Nick could smell toast and surely that wasn't bacon? He gave the guitar a final strum before laying it aside.

'How come you're not at work?' he asked, entering the kitchen.

Wearing track pants and a grey cotton top, hair pulled back, Dawn was breaking eggs into a bowl.

'They asked me if I'd switch shifts, just the next few days.' Balancing the egg shells in the palm of one hand, she dumped them in the bin beneath the sink. 'It means I could come with you when you have your stitches out.'

'They asked you to switch, or you asked them?'

'Don't you want me to come with you?'

'Not specially.'

Dawn pushed a loose hair away from her face, one that had slipped free. 'Scrambled eggs okay? Bacon?'

'Somebody's birthday, is it?'

'Don't be so cheeky.' She added a splash of milk and continued beating the eggs with a fork. 'Your dad used to say I made the best scrambled eggs he'd ever had.'

'He would, wouldn't he?'

'What do you mean by that?'

'Charlie said he could charm the birds down out of the trees if he wanted.'

'Charlie said.'

'Yes.'

'She should know.'

'Meaning?'

'It doesn't matter.'

Pulling out the grill pan, Dawn licked her fingers and quickly turned the bacon, then turned up the heat under the saucepan.

'Butter that toast for me, will you?'

She emptied the egg mixture into the melting butter and began to stir it round.

'She should know,' Nick repeated. 'What did you mean?'

'It doesn't matter, I said.'

'Were they . . . you know, my dad and Charlie?'

'It's all a long time ago.'

'But were they?'

'Yes, probably.'

'Is that why you don't like her?'

'I told you before, I do like her.'

'You don't like me seeing her though, do you?'

'Are you buttering that toast or not? These eggs are almost ready.'

'You don't, do you?'

'What you do's up to you.'

'Your face when I walked in from seeing her, it was all you could do not to burst out crying.'

Dawn lifted the pan off the gas. 'That wasn't anything to do with Charlie, you daft sod, that was you, waltzing in here with a guitar in your hand like you were him, years younger.'

'My dad?'

'Of course, your dad. You look just like him. Now pass those plates over here and sit yourself down. I didn't make this to see it get cold.'

For as long as it took them to clear their plates, neither spoke much beyond 'Pass the salt,' and 'Pass the sauce.'

Done, Dawn pushed her plate away and leaned back in her chair. 'Make us a cup of tea, there's a love.'

'I'll put the kettle on.'

'Don't strain yourself.'

Nick ran the water too fast, splashing it everywhere.

'Go careful.'

'It's only water.'

'That's not the point.'

What is then, Nick thought? 'Charlie and my dad,' he said, 'was it before you were seeing him or, you know, during?'

'God! What does it matter? After all this time.'

'It matters if I'm going to see her again, Charlie.'

'And are you?'

'I don't know. Maybe.'

'What for?'

'The guitar, she said she'd teach me.'

Dawn laughed. 'From what I just heard, somebody should.'

'Give us a chance.'

'I suppose I thought it might have come naturally. In the genes.'

The kettle started to boil and Dawn got to her feet. 'Come on, shift out of there and let me do that.'

'I know how to make tea, you know.'

'Suit yourself. I'll just rinse these things.'

'That pan wants soaking.'

'That your professional opinion?'

'If you like.'

Dawn squirted washing-up liquid into the bowl and turned on both taps. 'For what it's worth, I think anything between Les and Charlie was over well before he took up with me.'

'He carried on seeing her though.'

'They worked together, that's why. And they were friends. It is possible. Even if you've fancied one another.' Filling the small saucepan with water, she set it to one side. 'It's not all sex, you know.'

'I know.'

'Speaking of which . . .'

Nick looked at her warily, wondering what was coming.

'Mrs Rice, she said she saw you talking to this girl . . .'

'Which girl?'

'I don't know. Wearing a black beret, I think she said.'

Nick could feel himself going red.

'Struck a chord, have I?'

'Shut it!'

Dawn laughed. 'Who is she then?'

'Nobody.'

'That why you've gone the colour of beetroot?'

'Mum, for God's sake, leave it out.'

Dawn grinned. 'You see you do the same. Or else be careful.'

'Christ! All we've done is talk.'

'Yes, well. If it comes down to it, use a condom, that's all I'm saying.'

'I know what you're saying.'

'Good, now pour that tea before it gets stewed.'

Nick sighed and reached for the pot. If it comes down to it. Chance, he thought, would be a fine thing.

An hour later, Nick was sprawled across the settee, trying to concentrate on his book, when his mum appeared in the doorway in the orange overall she wore at work.

'I'm off.'

Nick grunted okay.

'That girl, the one with the beret, what did you say her name was?'

'Ellen.'

'Ellen. Hm, nice name. Don't study too hard.'

'Bye, mum.'

The door closed and Nick pushed himself up and crossed towards the TV. There was just so much of the Depression you could take in one go.

CHAPTER 19

'Okay,' Charlie said, 'that's right. Index finger on the third string, the G, and the next two fingers on the fourth and fifth. A fret lower, that's it. The D and the A. Now press down hard. Harder. Try and get your fingers close up behind the fret. Yes. Good thing you've got short nails, at least. All right, now bring the fingers of your other hand down across the strings. Don't be afraid of it. There, you see. E major. You're on your way.'

'God,' Nick said, moving his left hand away and giving it a shake.

'Don't worry,' Charlie said. 'It'll toughen up.'

'Yeah?'

'Yes. Now let's do something about the way you're sitting. Here, relax your shoulders, that's right. And bring this arm round so that your fingers – there – are more at less at right angles to the neck. Okay, don't flatten them. Don't flatten them. Good. Remember the positions? No, no. Yes, that's it. Good. Now – look, let me show you – there. That's it. Try for an even rhythm, count with me: one, two, three, four. Right, again. Yes, fine. You've got it. That's good. Now, still strumming, lift that finger from the D string – no, the D – right, and you've got E seventh. Hear the difference?'

When Nick had arrived at Charlie's house, carrying his guitar, she had been sitting on the front steps in a faded Fairport Convention t-shirt and a pair of baggy cords, repotting geraniums and fuschias.

'I should have done this weeks ago, but you know how it is. You put things off and you put things off.'

The pots stood on either side of the steps, orange terracotta, the flowers pink, purple, white and brick red, petals opening.

Charlie brushed the loose soil onto the scrap of garden beneath her window, picked up her trowel and green and white bag of multi-purpose compost and ushered Nick indoors.

'So,' she said, rinsing her hands beneath the tap. 'You really want to learn.'

'I think so.'

Charlie shook her head. 'Think so won't get it done. It takes time, effort, patience. Above all, patience. You think you've got that?'

Nick wasn't sure. 'Yes,' he said. 'Yes, I think so.'

'Good. Because otherwise you'll be wasting both our times, your and mine.'

Nick nodded. Why was she making it so hard? Hadn't it been her idea, after all?

'And you want to learn to play blues?' Charlie said.

'I suppose so,' Nick said, and then, hastily, intercepting her look, 'I mean, yes, yes, I do.'

'Good.'

After close to an hour, Nick had the first three basic positions down. E major, E minor, E seventh. What he couldn't quite manage while concentrating on that was to maintain a regular rhythm back and forth across the strings with his other hand, the basic boom-de, boom-de, boom-de, boom-de, four beats to the bar.

Tried and lost it.

Lost it and tried again.

'Take a break,' Charlie said.

'No, it's okay.'

'Nick, lighten up.'

'I thought you wanted me to take it seriously?'

'I do. But even Robert Johnson didn't learn it all in a day. No matter what they say about him selling his soul at the crossroads.'

Charlie knew she was letting him start off easy, no sense in pushing things too fast. Next time they'd cover A major and B seventh and Nick would be able to play a very basic twelve bar blues.

After a further ten minutes, Nick shook his head and laid the instrument aside. 'It's hard.'

'Of course it is.'

Nick was looking at the reddening indentations on his hand. 'Isn't there something you can do?

'What? You mean like wearing gloves? Baking them in the oven like conkers?'

Charlie made coffee and they sat close to the open window, one of the cats curled into a tight ball on the chair at Nick's back, two more book-ending the newly-filled flower box on the outside sill.

'That person you mentioned before,' Nick said. 'Robert Johnson? Special favourite of my dad's, was he?'

'Robert Johnson? Les liked him, of course. You'd have to. Anyone interested in the blues. Mississippi Delta blues especially. Country blues. Leadbelly. Blind Lemon Jefferson. Son House. But no, the ones your dad favoured were quieter, more subtle somehow, softer. Leroy Carr. Mississippi John Hurt. Skip James.

'Go into any decent record store nowadays and the racks are full of them. Cheap, too. But in those days, when these musicians were just being re-discovered, you could scarcely get hold of recordings for love or money. Dobells in Charing Cross Road, that was one place we used to go, fighting over anything decent, anything new. But then someone told Les about the record library at the American Embassy and he used to go along there, Grosvenor Square. Listen to all this Library of Congress stuff, American labels like Folkways.

'I think if things are more difficult to come by, like that, they seem more important. They were important to him, certainly. Some of the rest of us, we were just playing at it. Not Les.'

She picked up her mug of coffee with both hands.

Stuttering, the sounds of traffic travelling along Camberwell Road filtered across the square.

'You and my dad,' Nick began.

'What about us?'

'Were you, you know . . . ?'

'An item?'

'Yes, I suppose so.'

Charlie smiled, remembering. 'For a while, yes. A spell. He was beautiful, your dad. At least, I thought so.' She stared out across the street, a memory of Nick's father reflected against the trees. 'Of course, I wasn't the only one. But, I don't know, that time, when we were together. Six months it might have been, all told. They were special.'

She turned her head away so that he couldn't see her face.

Two kids went by on skate boards, heading for the park.

'I'll say one thing, though,' Charlie said, 'once he'd met your mum, once he'd met Dawn, that was it. He never looked at anyone else after that.' And then she laughed, a raw deep laugh. 'That's a lie, of course. I mean, he was a man, wasn't he? He looked. Wouldn't have been human if he didn't. Looked but didn't touch.'

'You're not just saying that?' Nick asked.

'And why ever would I do that?'

Nick shrugged. 'I don't know. Make me feel better, maybe. About him. Or you.'

Charlie shook her head. 'No, you could ask anyone. He really loved your mum. He really did. You too. You'd walk across the room, little more than three or four, and I could see his eyes following you.'

Nick set down his cup. 'Wasn't enough though, was it. Just wasn't bloody enough.'

Eyes smarting, he hurried from the room.

'Sometimes loving other people isn't enough, Nick,' Charlie said. 'You have to love yourself as well.'

If he heard her, she wasn't sure.

Alone in the other room, Nick picked up the guitar. First position, second, third, first, second, third. Four beats to the bar.

CHAPTER 20

There were seven Steves on the estate and during the course of twenty-four hours police officers spoke to them all. Of course, as Jackie Ferris well knew, the fact that Victoria Coleman had been attacked and robbed on the edge of the estate didn't necessarily mean that was where the perpetrators lived. For some, the old adage, don't mess on your own doorstep still held true. The criminals could have come from one of those nearby streets where flats were routinely bought and sold at prices in excess of three hundred thousand pounds and a family home cost upward of a million – the kind of street where Victoria Coleman herself lived and to which Jackie Ferris could never aspire.

Young offenders did come from those homes, but in Ferris's experience their crimes were more likely to involve drugs, drink, shoplifting, driving under the minimum age, driving without a licence, and a variety of offences under the Public Order Act of 1986. She even knew of one fourteen year old, whose father was a highly reputable barrister and whose mother was a successful civil liberties activist, who, after a number of ducks and swans had been found dead or dying on a local pond, had been arrested for – as the old law put it – cruelty to animals and for possession of parts of a crossbow which together (and without any other parts) could be assembled to form a crossbow capable of discharging a missile.

Not too many of the kids from those streets took to mugging strangers as a way of increasing their income or passing the time.

Whereas, in Jackie Ferris's eyes, the stereotype of the urban mugger was unfortunately close to the truth. Black or white, most street crime in the area was carried out by youngsters living on or within a half-mile radius of the estate. This estate and the many others like it. Don't mess on your own doorstep did not apply.

Of the seven Steves, three were already known to the police.

Of those, two had alibis for the evening in question.

Steve Johnson had been playing pool with his elder brother, Lawrence, his uncle Ryan and his uncle's friend, Pete. At around the time Victoria Coleman had found herself surrounded near the railway bridge, Steve had been failing to make a difficult shot off the cushion into the baulk pocket and earning a clip round the ear from his brother.

Steve Zephania had been grudgingly present at a special service at the Baptist church in Wood Green where his family worshipped.

Which left Steve Rawlings, sullen, cocky, so far in Ferris's face it was all she could do to keep her hands to herself. The two uniformed officers with her likewise.

'That woman got mugged, that's what this is about, i'n'it? Should've known better, shouldn't she? Walking through there. Stupid, i'n'it? Askin' for it.'

'And where were you, Steve?' Ferris asked, after counting slowly to ten inside her head.

'With my mates, weren't I?'

'Mates?'

'Yeah. Josh. Casper. Ross – Ross Blevitt. Ask him. Ask any of 'em.'

'And where was this?'

'Just, you know, around. Hangin' out.'

'All right,' Ferris said, 'let's go and see them, these friends of yours.' Knowing already it was a waste of time, but something that had to be gone through, something that had to be done.

Ross Blevitt wasn't too hard to find.

Lounging around the open space in front of the block where he lived with his stepfather and his brothers, the usual crew of seven or eight with him, smoking, joking, listening to what passed for music. Ferris's tastes ran more towards lounge stuff, easy listening, Andy Williams, Dean Martin, Stacey Kent – Amy Winehouse she could take at a pinch.

Blevitt flicked aside what remained of his cigarette, spat, and, hands in pockets, sauntered forwards, khaki sweat pants by 55DSL, striped t-shirt from Duffer of St George.

'Ross,' Ferris said, 'long time, no see. Must be a month at least since you were answering questions down at the station.'

'New regime,' Blevitt said and winked. 'New leaf.'

Standing behind and to one side, Rawlings laughed.

'The other night,' Ferris began . . .

'Woman got robbed,' Blevitt said. 'Cut, too. Nasty.'

'Rawlings here,' Ferris said, 'he claims he was with you.'

Blevitt's gaze shifted for a moment to where Rawlings was standing.

'He's lyin',' Blevitt said. 'Never saw him the whole evening. None of us did. Off somewhere with those mates of his, Casper an' that. Up to no good, I shouldn't wonder.'

'You bastard!' Rawlings said. 'You bastard.'

'Well, Steve,' Ferris said, turning towards him. 'It looks like you'll be coming down the station after all.'

The officers got hold of him firmly by both arms. Possibly firmer than was strictly necessary.

'Hey, Steve,' Blevitt called after them. 'That Stanley knife of yours. Still got it stashed somewhere?'

A police search of the Rawlings family flat produced no such weapon; by then it was at the bottom of the canal near Camden Lock.

What they did find, in a plastic sandwich bag taped inside the toilet cistern, was a gold necklace, identical to the one snatched from around Victoria Coleman's neck.

Before anyone could stop him, Rawlings' father, on a rare visit home, punched his son in the face and blacked his eye, broke his nose.

'All right,' Jackie Ferris said, 'That'll do,' thinking it was a shame Rawlings' old man hadn't tried something less severe but similar years before.

CHAPTER 21

The upside of his mum going to work late was she made breakfast, even if breakfast was only toast; the downside was he had to get up to eat it. Any suggestion she bring it to him in bed was sure to be greeted with enquiries as to what his last servant had died of and the like. The same remarks her mother, in turn, had made to her.

Even so, once Nick had pulled on some clothes and splashed water in his face, he didn't feel too bad. And the toast – not too thin, not too brown, butter and plenty of marmalade – the toast was good.

'That boy . . .' Dawn began.

'Which boy?' Nick said.

'The boy that mugged that woman with a knife . . .'

'Rawlings.'

'Yes. They reckon he might get sent away this time, borstal or wherever.'

Nick didn't think they had borstals any more. Or if they did, then they were called something else. 'Serve him right,' he mumbled and carried on eating.

'You know you're due at the hospital this morning?'

'No, I forgot. Clear slipped my mind.'

'Okay, you don't have to be sarcastic. I was just . . .'

'Getting on my case.'

'Reminding you.'

'Yeah, okay mum, thanks.'

'You sure you don't want me to come with you?'

A long-suffering look aside, Nick didn't bother with an answer.

Lifting the kettle, Dawn added warm water to the pot and swirled it round. 'You ready for some more tea?'

Nick pushed his cup towards her.

'You haven't seen Melanie lately, have you?' Dawn asked.

Nick shook his head.

'Nick, have you?'

'I said no, didn't I?'

'You shook your head.'

'Mum, it's a universally recognised sign, right? Movement of the head from side to side. It means no. No, I have not seen Melanie. Why would I?'

'I don't know. She went past in the street the other day, when I was working. Looked terrible, I thought.'

'She always looks terrible.'

'No, but I mean really terrible. Ill.'

Nick pushed away his plate. 'Okay, so take *her* to the hospital.'

'Very funny.'

'Or if you're so worried, go and ask her. Ask her mum.'

On balance, Dawn didn't think she'd bother; it rarely paid to interfere. She wanted a cigarette but rather than trigger another argument she thought she'd wait until she was alone.

'Nick, love, you wouldn't go down the corner and get us a paper, would you?'

'What did your last servant die of?'

'Kindness. Now, here you are . . .' Tipping change out of her purse. '*Mirror* or the *Mail*, I don't care which.'

With an ostentatious sigh, Nick palmed the money and left.

Dawn counted to ten, opened the kitchen window wide and lit up. It didn't escape her that she was the one behaving like a young teenager, sneaking fags behind grown-ups' backs.

Nick bumped into one of the boys from his class on the street, not someone he knocked around with, but knew well enough to talk to about the Arsenal and how much they hated Man U and how this other kid they both knew reckoned he'd shagged his cousin at her fourteenth birthday party.

At the shop he forgot and bought the *Sun* by mistake, knew his mum hated the *Sun* with a vengeance, wouldn't have it in the house, so took it back and changed it. He figured his mum

wouldn't care how long he was as long as she had
time to smoke one of her Benson's down to the
tip and spray air freshener round the kitchen.

'You had a phone call,' Dawn said, the moment
he came through the door.

'Chris?'

Dawn grinned. 'I don't think that's what she was
called.'

Nick could feel his cheeks starting to flush.

'It was Ellen. She said did you want to meet her
Saturday morning? Somewhere up the Archway.
The Toll Gate Café?'

Nick shrugged. 'I don't know.'

'Well, that's what she said, I'm sure.'

Nick's mouth felt dry. 'Is that all she said?'

'No,' Dawn said, grinning still. Loving this. 'She
said if you'll show her yours, she'll show you hers.'

Bright red, Nick dropped the newspaper on the
table, went into his room and closed the door.

The Toll Gate Café was marooned in the middle
of a large traffic island, along with a large pub, a
mini cab office, a second-hand clothes store and
little else. Getting there involved either waiting at
three different sets of lights, or taking your life in
your hands, vaulting some railings and running
like hell.

Nick chose the second option, rapped his ankle
on the top rail and was narrowly missed by a Ford
Fiesta, his art folder nearly slipping from his hand.

The place itself had curved windows, blue-green

paint and an old sign behind glass above the door, *Café Restaurant* in old-fashioned curvy script.

Nick pushed open the front door.

The interior was long and narrow, with mosaic tables and chairs in various shapes and sizes, some of which looked as if they'd been stripped from an old hall or cinema. There were paintings on the walls.

Emma was sitting half-way down, book open in front of her, folder propped alongside. She was wearing black cords and the same shirt she'd had on when he'd bumped into her in Camden, lavender blue. Head to one side, she was twisting a length of hair between her fingers as she read.

Music was playing, not loud. Nick vaguely recognised the song, without knowing either the lyrics or the singer. Something his mum might have known?

As Nick walked towards her, Ellen looked up from her book and smiled.

'Hi.'

'Hi.'

'What's wrong?'

'What d'you mean?'

'You're limping.'

'No, I'm not.'

'You are.'

'I banged my ankle,' Nick said. 'It's nothing.'

'Anyway,' Ellen said, 'you found it okay.'

'Yes.'

'You want coffee?'

'Sure.' Nick glanced along towards a serving area at the far end. Cakes and quiches. What looked like fruit salad. A coffee machine. 'Do they . . . ?'

Ellen shook her head. 'You order there, they bring it here.'

'What's that?' he asked, pointing at the tall glass by her arm.

'Latté.'

Nick left his folder on the table and went to place his order. There was one woman in front of him, a small child, a baby, little more, asleep in a sling close to her chest. A bearded man reading the newspaper aside, most of the other customers seemed to be mothers with children. At the very back, an Asian guy, not so much older than Nick himself, was working away at his laptop.

By the time, he got back to the table, Ellen had his folder open and was leafing through the contents.

'Some of this is really great.'

'Oh, yeah, fine. Don't wait to be asked.'

'I'm sorry.'

'No, it's okay.'

'I mean, I thought that was the point.'

'It is, it is.'

'So?'

Nick sat down and re-angled the folder between them. 'Go on, then.'

'What?'

'Tell me what you liked.'

Ellen leaned back in her creaky chair. 'I like the

idea. I really like the idea. The maps and all that. And some of the photos. Here . . .' Leaning forward again, delving. 'This one, for instance. Brilliant, yeah?'

Nick flushed with pleasure.

In the photograph, a burly stall-holder, red-faced, chest hair sprouting from his open shirt, was waving an outsize purple aubergine in the direction of two Muslim women clad from head to toe in black, dark eyes all that were visible, wide in surprise.

'Okay,' Nick said, 'so why d'you like it?'

'It's funny for a start. The bloke, he's like those blokes in those old seaside postcards. Sort of like a caricature, you know. Not real. Except he is. And the women . . . the way they're looking at him . . . it's the whole thing about, you know, society. Multicultural. No, I love it. It's great.'

A waitress brought Nick's latté and found space for it on the table.

'What about the rest?' Nick asked.

Ellen made a face. 'The paintings,' she said. 'Well, they're not very good, are they?'

'Says who?'

'Says me.' Laughing. 'I'm sorry, Nick. They've got to go.'

'All right, genius.' Starting to reach across her. 'Let's see yours.'

'In a minute. We haven't finished looking at this yet.'

'It's all crap, remember.'

'Not all.'

'Apart from the man with the aubergine.'

'Apart from the man with the aubergine.'

Nick leafed through several sheets until he found what he was looking for: several pictures of giant boot and shoes hanging high over the shops below. 'Here. What about these?'

'They're okay.'

'Only okay?'

'Yes, you know, you've seen them before.'

'Of course you have, they're there.'

'I mean everyone that goes down Camden, that's what they take pictures of, those stupid shoes.'

'Well, I'm sorry,' Nick said, flapping the folder shut and turning away.

'Oh, come on,' Ellen said, 'don't get like that.'

'I'm not like anything.'

'You're sulking.'

'I'm not.'

But when he looked at her and the way she was smiling, just with her eyes, he shook his head and grinned. 'Maybe just a bit.'

'If I just went ahead and said everything was wonderful . . . well, what's the point?'

'I know.'

'And I do like a lot of it, I really do.'

'You said. Except the paintings are useless and these are too.'

He pulled one of the photos from the page and tore it in half then half again.

'Nick!'

'What?' A second photo torn across and then a third.

'Stop.'

'Why? They're crap.'

Ellen stared at him, unsure of how angry he really was. After a moment, she reached out a hand to touch his forehead. 'Your stitches, you've had them out.'

'Yesterday.'

'There's just a little scar.'

'Yes, I know.'

'It'll fade.'

'Probably.'

She was slow taking her hand away. 'I like it,' she said. 'Your scar.'

'Thanks.'

'Your photos . . .' she said.

'No,' Nick said. 'Not now. Let's look at yours instead.'

Almost immediately he could see why she thought his painting was poor.

The first section of the folder was portraits, head and shoulders, mostly. Several girls, a couple of whom Nick recognised as being from her school. And the bloke, the DJ she'd been going out with he assumed, black face smiling, serious, handsome. Nick didn't ask and she didn't say.

Next were what he supposed were still lives: groups of ordinary things clustered on a dressing table around a vase of flowers. Girls' things.

Lipstick. Lotion. Lip salve. A box of tampons half-hidden by a magazine.

'Careful,' Ellen said, when he came to the back of the folder. 'Sometimes it sticks.'

As Nick lifted the page a picture opened out on three sides like something from a children's book. Except this was a collage of photographs Ellen had cut from magazines. Images from the Iraq war, bombed buildings, falling statues, burned-out tanks, charred bodies. And curling out of these she had painted tiny flowers, budding leaves, tendrils of green.

Nick couldn't quite look at her. 'It's brilliant,' he said.

'It's not focussed, like yours.'

'It's brilliant,' he said again.

'If you don't drink that latté soon,' she said, 'it'll be stone cold.'

CHAPTER 22

'Who's this again we're going to see?' Nick asked.

They were going up the escalator at Leicester Square.

'Walker Evans,' Ellen said. 'Well, not him exactly.' Smiling. 'He's dead, I'm pretty sure.'

Talking to Ellen, Nick was beginning to wonder what he'd been doing with his life. There she was, rattling on about Tate Modern this, Tate Britain that, taking courses with students from some College of Art or other and charging about all over London at weekends, and if ever he strayed beyond his particular patch it was to go to the Emirates, and that was no more than a short ride on a number 4 bus.

'Here,' Ellen said. 'This way.'

The interior of the tube station was busy with people hurrying in every direction, a good number of them, Nick noticed, Chinese.

He followed Ellen up two flights of steps and out on to the street.

The Photographers' Gallery was just across the road.

Nick wondered if you had to pay, but it seemed not. The glass door pushed back and they were inside. Photographs hung along both walls, the gallery narrow at first and then opening out. Nick didn't think he'd seen so many photos in one place before.

Ellen had walked on a little way ahead of him and Nick, turning, saw what looked like some kind of an introduction on the wall. He didn't read all of it, but enough to get the gist. A lot of the photographs had been taken with a Polaroid camera when Evans was pretty old, the rest were from earlier in his career.

And he was American, Walker Evans, Nick hadn't realised that.

His first break had come in the thirties, the Depression – like, who was it? – Dorothea Lange. Except that while she was following the Okies out to California, Evans was in the South. Mississippi.

Wasn't that where Charlie said his dad's favourite singers had come from?

The Mississippi Delta. Mississippi Delta Blues.

'What you doing?' Ellen was standing beside him, her arm touching his.

'Nothing. Reading this.'

'I wanted to show you something.'

Unlike the older photographs, which were all in black and white, the Polaroids were in colour.

160

Small squares of colour at the centre of glass frames, arranged in groups on the wall.

Some were of shop fronts, not the whole thing, just part. Boots, scarves and gloves with their prices attached. Newspapers on a stand. Books and all kinds of things spread along the pavement for sale, just like you'd see in Camden or on the Holloway Road. A sign which made him snigger: *Do Not Hump*. Arrows on the surface of the road. Fly-posters. The broken windows of old abandoned cars. 'There must be twenty or more like that,' Nick said. 'All round the Estate.' Signs fading above shop windows. Parts of letters. A **B** and half a **U**. A large **E** next to the beginnings of an **S**.

Bits and pieces.

What Evans had liked about the Polaroid camera, Nick had read, it made him focus on just parts of things.

In a cabinet, protected by glass, were some of the magazines in which a lot of the pictures had first been seen. Above them the words: *Before they Disappear*.

'What do you think?' Ellen asked.

'About what?'

'This. This stuff.'

'I like it.'

In the shop, Nick leafed through a fat book of photographs on the table. Glossy paper that felt shiny and smooth.

'You're kidding,' he said, when he looked at the price on the back.

And there were others, thirty, forty pounds; twenty-nine pounds, ninety-five.

He bought a couple of postcards, one showing the interior of a room in 1933, the other a number of signs hanging up outside a wooden building – *Fish Co., Fruits Vegetables, Art School.*

'You want to go round again?' Ellen asked.

'Later. Can we do it later? Too much now'd do my head in.'

They wandered up through Chinatown and past a cinema showing films Nick had never heard of, Ellen making him wait while she went into a fancy cake shop and bought a chocolate eclair.

The benches in Soho Square were all taken, so they sat on the grass and passed the eclair between them, impossible to prevent the cream oozing between their fingers. The way the light came through the trees meant that while Nick's face was partly in shadow, Ellen had to shield her eyes from the sun.

Nick would never be able to remember, no matter how hard he tried, exactly which of them made the first move nor how it was they were kissing. Except that they were.

And all around them no one cared.

'Do you really want to go back and look at the photos?' Ellen asked after a while.

Nick shook his head. 'No. Do you?'

'So how did it go?' His mum asked when he got home. 'Have a nice time?'

'Yeah,' Nick said quickly. 'Okay.'

And disappeared into his room.

CHAPTER 23

Sunday morning Nick got up early. The camera he'd borrowed from Christopher, who'd got it from his father, was an old Cannon EOS with a zoom lens. Nick had fiddled about with the lens before and ended up hardly ever using it, but now, after seeing the Walker Evans, he thought it might have its uses.

Get in close.

Look. Look up.

Before they Disappear.

He started at the Toll Gate Café, the sign above the door. Focussed on the letters, first one, then two, then more. Finally decided on **Rest** with the **t** not quite in the frame.

On the pavement near the tube station, a whole lot of different Irish papers were on display, and, mingled amongst them, *Le Monde* and several others in Italian and Spanish and what Nick thought was probably Arabic.

Walking along Fortess Road, he noticed workmen had pulled away the boards above the Internet Café, revealing partially faded white letters. FRENCH & ENGLISH CONFECTIONERS. How long they'd been there, he'd no idea. He'd certainly never seen them before.

Cutting through, he took some pictures of graffiti on the bridge over the railway, before finding himself staring at what he must have walked past half a hundred times before but never really noticed. Across the courtyard from the pub, high on the side wall of what was now a hair salon, the name of the shop's previous owners had been painted directly onto the brick, and, listed underneath, the things that they'd sold.

```
 K & M LARN
FANCY WORK
OVERALLS
BLOUSES
CORSETS
GLOVES
HOSIERY
LACES
RIBBONS
HABERDASHERY
FLANNELS
FLANNELETTES
CALICOES
UNDERCLOTHING
MAIDS' DRESSES
CAPS & APRONS
```

Here and there, the lettering had faded into the brickwork to the point that it was unreadable without the rest of the word to make sense. When had they first been put there, Nick wondered? A hundred years ago? Possibly more. And the words themselves. What on earth was haberdashery, for instance? And what were calicoes?

The Flannelettes sounded like one of those sixties girl groups on the cheap compilation CDs his mum brought back sometimes from the petrol station where she worked.

Standing there, zooming in and out, really getting into it, he took shot after shot until he realised with surprise the film was finished and he didn't have another.

He was close enough to Christopher's to call round there, but Sunday morning he knew Chris would still be stewing in his bed and wouldn't appreciate being knocked awake.

He got home just as his mum was emerging from the bathroom, bleary-eyed, tatty old dressing gown pulled tight around her.

'Where've you been this early?'

She moved past him, intent on filling the kettle, making a cup of tea.

'Mum, lend us some money.'

'What for?'

'What does it matter?'

'Of course it matters.'

'Mum . . .'

After rummaging round in her bag, she came

up with some change and a five pound note. 'Until I can get to a machine, that's all I've got.'

'Should've taken it easy last night then, eh?'

'What do you know about what I did or didn't do last night?'

'Nothing,' Nick said. The longer his mum's private life remained private the better. Once in a while when she went out with her friends on a Saturday, he'd be vaguely aware of her returning home at three or so in the morning. Once he got up at five to go for a pee and came face to face with her sneaking in through the front door.

The fiver was still in Dawn's hand.

'I'll pay you back,' Nick said.

'I know you will.'

'So come on then, give it over.'

'If it's condoms . . .'

'What? You gonna lend me yours?'

'Don't be so damned cheeky.'

'What is it with you, anyway? You got condoms on the brain?'

'Fat lot of good they'd do you there.'

'Funny! Highly satirical. Been watching *Have I Got News For You?* again?'

'I just don't want you getting some girl into trouble, that's all.'

'I tell you what, mum. You look after your sex life, I'll look after mine.'

'Dawn laughed. 'That includes washing your own sheets then, does it?'

'Okay,' Nick said, turning away to hide his face. 'Keep your money.'

'Here. You want it? Here.'

Leaving the note on the table, she turned back towards the kettle. 'Fancy a cup of tea before you go wherever it is you're going?'

'No, thanks.'

Nick pocketed the fiver, picked up the camera and left.

When the man in shop from whom he bought the film showed an interest and asked him what he was doing, he asked Nick if he'd ever looked at the rear of the buildings at the far side of the roundabout, near the entrance to the Fields.

Nick had not.

'You know where that greasy spoon used to be? All tarted up now.'

Nick nodded.

'Round the back of there.'

'Okay, thanks. I'll go and look now.'

Through the overlapping branches, he could just make out the writing on the wall, in danger of disappearing into the reddish brick.

CATERING
  FOR
BEANFEASTS
 PARTIES
 CLUBS

Beanfeasts, Nick thought, what a great word. He grinned at the thought of a hundred or so help-ings of baked beans on toast and all the farting that would follow. Forget windmills, harness that lot and there'd be power enough to keep the electricity supply going for weeks.

Then again, maybe it meant something else.

He was just turning away when he saw Melanie – or someone he thought was Melanie – walking across the grass in the direction of the ponds. Head down, collar up, moving slowly. Trudging, that was the word. Something about the way she was walking made him call her name, but if she heard it she gave no sign.

Nick shrugged and passed between the metal barriers and back on to the main road. The smell of breakfasts cooking from the café made him long for a bacon sandwich, but he didn't think there was change enough from his five pound note, not for that and something to drink to wash it down.

He'd go home instead and raid the fridge. See what he could find.

Dawn was in the living room, vacuum cleaner going full blast, the radio still on in the kitchen.

'. . . police are still trying to trace the where-abouts of a one-day old baby, abandoned yesterday evening outside The Whittington Hospital on Highgate Hill. The baby, a boy weighing just under five pounds, is being cared for by staff at the hospital, who have named him Angus.'

Cold spread along Nick's arms like a wave.

Pushing past his mum, almost tripping over the lead from the Hoover, he switched on the TV and searched for the remote, which, as usual, had slipped down between the cushions on the settee.

'What's got into you all of a sudden?' Dawn asked.

Ignoring her, Nick flicked to CFax, continuing till he found the appropriate page.

'Baby Angus, the boy abandoned by his mother in the grounds of The Whittington Hospital in north London, was pronounced fit and healthy by staff this morning.

'A member of the public has reported seeing a young woman hurrying away from the spot where the baby was found. She is described as white, in her teens or possibly early twenties, and quite heavily-built.

'Detective Inspector James Mulwhinney, of Islington police, has appealed to the mother to contact either the Islington Child Protection Unit or the police as soon as possible.

'"I must emphasise," Inspector Mulwhinney said, "that our primary consideration at this time is the health and welfare of the mother, who may be in urgent need of medical attention."'

Phone numbers for the Child Protection Unit and the Islington police came up on the screen as Nick hurried back out of the room.

'Nick. Nicky. For heaven's sake what's going on?'

The slamming of the front door was her only reply.

CHAPTER 24

Nick ran when he could, walked when he couldn't. Midway along the first path leading into the Fields, he leaned forward against a bench to catch his breath. The soreness, where his ribs were far from fully healed, was intense.

A young woman, it had said, heavily-built. 'Our primary consideration at this time is the health and welfare of the mother, who may be in urgent need of medical attention.'

Whatever happened would more than likely have already happened.

No need to run.

And yet, following the path as it curved towards the first pond, he broke into a slow, steady jog, remembering Melanie as she had stood red-eyed at his door: 'I just . . . just wanted someone to talk to.'

The door closing in her face.

The water on the surface of the pond was calm, no dogs splashing noisily after frisbees or pieces of wood, no clamour of ducks as toddlers threw them hunks of bread. Out near the centre, two swans described a slow circle, a brace of darker-feathered cygnets close between. Once Nick had seen an adult swan, enraged, see off a dog which had swum too close to its young, the swan's wings thrashing the water furiously as it chased the intruder away.

At the next open pond there was more activity: men fishing, four or five at intervals; women pushing three-wheeled buggies along the gravelled path; near the far end, a father and child, a boy or girl, Nick couldn't tell, were sailing a small boat with orange sails.

What had he expected?

Melanie's coat floating, sodden, on top of the water where she had jumped in?

It wasn't everyone's solution, every person's escape.

Beyond the couple with the sailboat, he saw someone sitting on the grass, head bowed, arms tight around her knees. The shape was right, but as he got nearer, Nick could see it was someone else.

He was beginning to feel foolish.

Why not go home, phone one of those numbers? The Child Protection Unit. Or better still, do nothing. After all, it wasn't really his concern.

The sun showed through streaks of cloud as he climbed the angled path towards Parliament Hill, kites in different shapes and sizes moving against the sky, the largest, in the shape of a dragon's head, soaring as it caught the wind.

Nick stood for a while and watched. Below him, on the other side of the hill, was the running track where, on sports day, he had run his first hundred metres and almost won; alongside it, the play-ground where his father had first pushed him on the swings and where, falling from the climbing frame, he had bloodied both his knees. His father . . .

Walking down, he saw her, Melanie, sitting inside the shell of the bandstand, her back against the iron railing.

She scarcely moved when he came towards her. Only when he was standing in front of her did she look up and then quickly back down.

'Melanie,' Nick said. 'Are you okay?'

No reply and he knew, as soon as the words had left his mouth, what a stupid question it was. But he couldn't think what else to say.

He squatted down and waited until she looked at him again.

Her skin was pale and bagged around the eyes and the eyes themselves were dark and dull. Her coat seemed damp in patches, bits of twig and leaf clinging to it here and there as if maybe she had pushed her way into the undergrowth beyond the trees.

'Let me get you something,' Nick said.

'No.'

There was a café near the bandstand; he and Christopher and Scott used to go there all the time, until one day, without reason, they'd stopped and starting going somewhere else. The pizza place.

'Something to eat. A cup of tea.'

'I couldn't eat.'

'Cup of tea then.'

'All right.'

He had money enough left for two teas and a packet of biscuits in case she changed her mind about eating. He hurried back, fearful that she might have gone, but she was still in the same position.

A small boy was climbing round the other side of the bandstand now, negotiating the spaces between the railings with care, his mother watching closely lest he should fall.

Nick set down the cups on the floor and sat at Melanie's side.

From his pocket he took several packets of sugar and a small plastic spoon.

'How many? One? Two?'

'Three.'

They sat for a while and sipped their tea. The small boy was replaced by an inquisitive dog.

'The baby . . .' Nick began.

'Don't,' Melanie said.

'I just wanted . . .'

'Don't.'

Nick offered Melanie a biscuit and when she shook her head, he took one himself and dunked it in the tea. The dog came sniffing close and Nick aimed a kick to keep it away.

Someone had once told him that you only heard birds early in the mornings and late in the afternoons. What he could hear now was the sound of traffic, distant on the main road, the occasional voices from outside the café, Melanie's breathing as she sat, her arm not quite touching his.

'I didn't know what else to do,' she said suddenly, her voice hushed but rough, as if her throat were sore. 'I tried to tell my mum, I mean when I knew. No way I could have told my dad, no way. He'd have killed me. I know. And my mum, I just don't know what she'd have done. Panicked most likely and told him anyway. Forced me to have an abortion, I don't know. So I just carried on, tried to pretend it wasn't happening I suppose. And then . . . no, no, it doesn't matter. You don't want to hear all this. You don't have to.'

'No,' Nick said. 'Go on. I do.'

Slowly she looked at him. 'Why are you saying that?'

'Because it's true.'

She picked up her tea but didn't drink it. 'I was in the bathroom. My mum was out. I knew something was going to happen. All this water . . . and then these pains. I locked the door and at first I sat on the toilet, I didn't know what to do, and then I got into the bath. I . . .'

She stopped, tears welling up, and Nick squeezed her arm.

'I thought I can't, I can't. I couldn't believe the pain. Shouting and screaming, I don't know why

176

someone in the other flats didn't hear me and then, suddenly, there he was. Small and red and all wrinkled and at first I didn't want to touch him, couldn't bring myself to, but that was only a moment, a couple of moments, and then I picked him up and as soon as I did he started crying and opened his eyes and looked at me . . .'

'Sshh,' Nick said. 'It's okay.'

'I knew I had to get a knife, to cut, you know, the cord, and I left all this . . . all this blood and stuff all over the kitchen floor. I ran the tap over the scissors until it was boiling hot and then I cut it and he was still crying so I wrapped him up in these towels, they were clean, just washed, and found this holdall and I took him . . . I could hardly walk, it hurt, but I took him to the hospital. I thought it would be best for him and I didn't want anyone to know.'

She grabbed his hand and gripped it tight.

The last of her words had been almost lost in tears.

'It's okay, it's okay,' Nick said over and over, praying no one would come near.

After a while, Melanie released his hand and wiped the sleeve of her coat across her face.

'Nick, I've done a terrible thing, haven't I? A wicked thing.'

'No,' Nick said. 'I don't think so.'

And a little while later Nick got to his feet and said, 'If you want to go home or to the hospital or whatever, I'll come with you. If you want.'

Melanie shook her head. 'I think I'd like to just stay here. For a bit longer.'

'Okay,' Nick said, and sat back down beside her.

Later, in his own room that evening, when the fuss, most of it, had died down, and Nick was stretched out on his bed, eyes closed, he heard his father's voice.

'You did well, son, today. Made it right, right as you could. I like to think I'd've done the same.'

Of course, when he opened his eyes there was no one there.

CHAPTER 25

'So what happened then?' Ellen asked. 'To Melanie?'

It was almost a week later, and they were sitting by one of the round windows at the front of the Toll Gate Café. The prints of Nick's photographs were on the table, but that wasn't what they were talking about.

'She agreed to come back with me,' Nick said. 'Eventually. Talk to my mum. She wouldn't go near her own. Not then. Mum persuaded her to go to the hospital.'

'And was she all right?'

'I think so. They kept her in overnight, I don't know, tests or something, observation, I'm not sure. But, yeah, I think she was okay.'

'And the baby?'

'Social services.'

'She's not going to keep her? Melanie?'

Nick shook his head. 'Going to have it put up for adoption, mum reckoned.'

'If it had been me . . .' Ellen began and then left it hanging. 'You don't know who the father is?' she said.

'No.'

'When you were talking to her, she didn't say?'

'No.'

Ellen stirred her latté, spreading the darker coffee up the glass.

'Let's have a look at these,' she said, spreading the photographs across the table. 'How many are you going to use?'

'I don't know yet.'

'You can't use all of them.'

'I know that.'

'This one,' Ellen said, lifting it up carefully with middle finger and thumb, 'you've got to have this.'

It was a close-up showing part of an old-fashioned shop window in Kentish Town, done out as if Next and Top Shop had never existed. Dresses Nick couldn't imagine anyone wearing let alone buying, each with its price clearly marked and some comment hand-written onto card – *New Season's Colours – Latest Fashion*.

'You don't think it's too like the one we saw?'

'The Walker Evans?'

'I don't want to get marked down for copying.'

Ellen grinned. 'Call it an *homage*. That's what artists do when they nick stuff from others. Your teacher'll probably think it's cool.'

Nick hoped she was right.

When they got outside it was threatening rain. On the pavement outside the Archway Tavern, a sandy-haired man in baggy trousers and a suit jacket but no shirt was playing the penny whistle. Traffic seemed to have come to a standstill in every direction.

'You know this afternoon,' Ellen said above the sound of car horns. 'I said I thought we might go and see this film . . .'

Oh-oh, Nick thought, here it comes.

'Well, my dad's coming home. Unexpectedly. I haven't seen him in ages.'

Ellen's father, Nick knew, was a doctor working in Zimbabwe or Namibia or somewhere. He couldn't remember what she'd said.

'We're all going to go out and meet him at the airport.'

'Yeah,' Nick said.

'I'm really excited.'

'Yeah.' If she was so excited, why hadn't she mentioned it before?

'Nick, you don't mind?'

'Why should I?'

Ellen shook her head and sighed. 'Look, I have to go.'

'Okay.'

He stood, rooted, as she started to walk away. She was almost at the crossing before he called after her. 'When will I see you?'

'Call me. You've got my number, right?'

'Right.' It was written inside the back cover of his folder.

He watched as she slipped between the lanes of

stationery cars, arms swinging lightly, trade mark beret angled back on her head. At the far side of the road, people milling round her, she raised her hand to wave.

By the time Nick had waved back she was lost to sight.

Back home, he rang the place where he worked and checked it would be okay to start back again at the end of the week. Christopher wasn't answering his mobile, which probably meant he'd forgotten to charge the batteries. Scott and Laura were at the Holloway Odeon, he knew, watching something or other.

'Why don't you come with us?' Scott had asked.

'No, it's okay.'

'Come on.'

'Leave him,' Laura had said, something of a leer on her face. 'Nick's got other things to do now, haven't you, Nick?'

Not so's you'd notice, Nick thought.

In his room, he lifted down the guitar and began to work his way, laboriously, through the three basic chords in E.

Half an hour later, less, the fingers on his left hand were starting to get sore and he was bored. Played at the only speed he could manage, it didn't sound much like music. It didn't sound much like anything.

Out in the kitchen he tried Christopher's number again. Nothing.

TV offered a film about Bonnie Prince Charlie, rowing, *Home and Away*, a John Wayne western or racing from Newmarket, Windsor and Musselburgh.

On the floor beside his bed *The Grapes of Wrath* lay accusingly closed.

He fished out his father's tape and set it to play.

Lay back on the bed and closed his eyes.

Feelin' tomorrow like I feel today
If I'm feelin' tomorrow like I feel today
Gonna pack my trunk an' make my getaway

Worried, baby, trouble in mind
Yes, I'm worried, baby, got trouble in mind
Never satisfied, just can't keep from cryin'

Whatever his father had been feeling, whatever had been worrying him, getting him down, whatever he had felt unable to face, Nick still couldn't really understand.

What had Charlie said? Sometimes loving other people isn't enough, you have to love yourself as well.

His mum had said he was afraid.

The track came to an abrupt end and another started part-way through.

Hard luck's at your front door, blues are in your
  room
Hard luck is at your front door, blues all round
  your room
Blues at your back door, what's gonna become of
  you?

Nick pushed himself off the bed and reached for his jacket, scribbled a note to his mum and left it on the kitchen table.

By the time he arrived the lunch rush was over and Marcus was standing out back with a cigarette in one hand, a bottle of imported Anchor Steam in the other.

'I thought you said next weekend?'

'I did.'

'So?'

'So I felt like working, that's all.'

Marcus let smoke drift upwards from the corner of his mouth. 'Too early for the evening shift, you know that.'

'That's okay, there must be something I can do.'

'There's pans in soak. A sack of potatoes that wants peeling.'

'Okay.'

'You know the money's the same?'

'Yeah.'

'And you'll work right through?'

'Yes.'

'You've had lunch?'

Nick shook his head.

'Get something first. Don't want you fainting on the job.'

Nick grinned and headed back inside.

CHAPTER 26

Steve Rawlings had a piece of tape across the bridge of his nose, helping him to breath. There was residual bruising, slow to fade, beneath his right eye. The knuckles of his left hand were newly raw.

Less than an hour before, just a few hours after he'd done a bunk from the supposedly secure unit he'd been sent to, Rawlings had followed a fourteen-year old drug dealer into the car park of a block of flats behind the Holloway Road and attacked him with a brick. Hit him so hard and so often there were spots of blood dark across his t-shirt and brick dust embedded in the palm and fingers of his right hand.

Something well satisfying, Rawlings thought, hitting someone with the broken half of brick.

Almost more satisfying than cutting them with a blade.

How about more than using a gun?

As yet he didn't know.

He thought he might find out.

Murray had told him about the gun inside, the pair of them cooped up in a poky top floor room, bars on the windows and locks on the doors. Told him how Bradley – that was the kid Rawlings had just whacked with the brick – worked between the scuzzy park outside the leisure centre and the flats. Hand signals and mobile phones. Told him how Bradley, ever since he'd been lost his stash to some blokes in a pumped-up Sierra from south of the river, always carried a gun.

An air pistol converted to fire .22 ammunition. Brocock ME38 Magnum.

Bradley braving it out at fourteen, a year and a bit less than Rawlings himself.

It had cost him a hundred quid, back of a pub in Willesden.

'I don't want no air pistol,' Rawlings had said. 'Think I'm some kid or what?'

But when Murray assured him just such a weapon had killed an Asian taxi driver in Bradford, he thought it might be okay just the same.

Right now it felt good in Rawlings' hand.

And as he got close to the estate, it felt good tucked down into his belt beneath his t-shirt and his Nike top, cold against the small of his back.

He would call Casper on the mobile he'd taken along with the gun: call Casper and let him get hold of Harry and Josh.

The gun and the mobile weren't the only things Rawlings had boosted. By the time the four of them left Harry Leroy's flat they were pretty high. Leroy's mum working somewhere round Finsbury Park – no questions asked – and his dad finishing eighteen months inside.

Leroy's mum had been foolish enough to leave around an almost full bottle of cheap vodka and Josh had gone down to the corner shop for a couple of six-packs of beer.

They hit the walkway loud and crazy, pushing one another from side to side, laughing at Harry's infirm attempt to impersonate Biggie Smalls.

Smack into Ross Blevitt and half a dozen others, sauntering their way down to the Boston for a game of pool.

'Shit!' Josh said and nobody else said a word.

After a moment, Rawlings pushed back his hood and started to walk to where Blevitt stood. Blevitt, wearing his usual Burberry cap, waiting with amusement in his eyes.

'What's up?' Blevitt said. 'Thought you was all tucked up inside.'

'You grassed me up,' Rawlings said. 'Turned me in.'

Blevitt smiled. 'Man, you grass yourself up, right? Every time you open your stupid mouth.'

'Yeah?'

'Yeah. You an' your pathetic little crew. Look at 'em, standin' there pissin' their pants.'

Laughter from Blevitt's friends, fingers pointing, gestures miming masturbation, fists.

'What you gonna do now,' Blevitt asked. 'Find another girl to beat up, all by yourselves?'

Angry, Rawlings came a step closer, one step then another. 'You'll find out, right? Soon enough.'

'Ooh,' Blevitt laughed. 'Scary!'

Rawlings reached round behind and brought out the gun.

'Jesus!' someone said.

All watching as, hand not quite steady, Rawlings aimed the gun at Blevitt's chest.

'What'm I supposed to do now?' Blevitt said. 'Get down on my knees? Pray?' And laughed in Rawlings' face. 'You know what? You're too chicken, i'n'it? Pussy, yeah?'

Contempt on his face, he slowly turned and began to walk, slowly, away.

Finger close to the trigger, Rawlings straightened his arm and took aim.

Five metres, ten, fifteen. Rawlings aware of everyone staring at him. His arm starting to shake.

Blevitt, never bothering to look back, was now thirty metres off and about to move out of sight.

Sweat ran down into Rawlings' eyes.

'Big deal,' he said, lowering his arm. 'Bastard's all mouth, right?' And then, as he headed back along the walkway. 'Better things to do, yeah?'

Lamont and Handley had heard the message on their radio, earlier in the day: Steven Rawlings, absconded from local authority care.

'Isn't that the lad went for that woman with a knife?' Lamont said.

'The same.'

'Let's stick close to the estate then. His sort, they never stray far from home.'

'Okay,' Handley said, wondering which course her partner had learned that on.

A little shy of ten, they were turning left out of the lights on Gordon House Road, when Lamont, driving, noticed four youths crossing towards the petrol station on the opposite corner.

'What d'you reckon?'

'Just kids.'

'Well,' Lamont said, turning the wheel. 'Won't hurt to take a look.'

That time of evening the petrol station was usually pretty quiet. Those motorists who filled up on their way home had long been and gone and the late night rush, such as it was, was still to start. Just a few lone cars, one every ten minutes or so, no more; a handful of locals nipping in for a loaf of bread, a pint of milk. Dawn wondered how much longer the owners were going to think it worthwhile opening evenings at all. Closing at eight might be better, eight-thirty at a pinch.

She always kept a magazine close by the counter, *Hello* or *Okay*, something to stop the time dragging, but by now she was up to here with who'd married whom and who was wearing what, and was stacking cans in the chiller cabinet, bending low, practically kneeling, when the boys came in.

'No one here,' she heard one of them say.

Then one of the others, 'Shut it!'

When she stood up the one who'd spoken last told her to get back over to the till and give them all the money she'd got. He was holding a gun.

Lamont drove past the petrol station on the opposite side of the road, did a U-turn and brought the vehicle to a standstill some three or four car-lengths short.

'What now?' Handley said.

Lamont shrugged. 'Go in and take a look.'

'You wait here,' Handley said, releasing her seat belt. 'I need some more mints. I'll go.'

'Suit yourself.'

Inside, no one had moved.

'You deaf,' Rawlings said, 'or what?' Jabbing the gun barrel towards Dawn's face.

'No, no. I just . . .'

'Then get over there. Now.'

Something about the gun, Dawn thought, didn't look right and she wondered if it might be a replica; wondered without wanting to put it to the test.

'Move it!'

'Okay, okay.' Trying to keep the fear out of her voice.

She was almost at the till when she saw a

uniformed policewoman crossing the forecourt towards the door.

At almost the same moment, Diane Handley saw Dawn looking in her direction and read the concern, the warning on her face; saw the way the youths were standing round her; saw, or thought she saw, the gun.

'What?' Rawlings said. 'What's wrong?'

'N . . . nothing,' Dawn stumbled.

'Then open it up. And you,' pointing at Josh, 'get those fags. Put 'em in a bag. Come on, do it now. Casper, what's the fuckin' matter with you? I tell you to keep watch or what?'

Handley made it back to the car without being seen.

'Armed robbery in progress. Call it in.'

When the message went back out from the control centre, logged Immediate, Jackie Ferris was sitting in her own car in Kentish Town, round the corner from Nandos, radio tuned to the police channel, eating peri-peri chicken and chips.

An armed response vehicle carrying two authorised firearms officers was closer, only minutes away, having been called to a brawl at a pub in Queen's Crescent.

Dawn breathed out slowly and evenly, pressed a button and the till sprang open.

'Okay,' Rawlings said. 'Empty it. The notes, the notes, just the notes. Come on.'

Dawn fumbled, letting some of the money slip from her fingers, playing for time as best she could.

Rawlings threatening, cursing, the rest of them more and more nervous. Harry Leroy, sober now, straight and sober, wishing to hell he wasn't there, close to making a run for it, worried only about what Rawlings would do.

Casper backed into the centre aisle and tins of lubricating oil went tumbling.

'Okay,' Rawlings said, snatching the last of the notes. 'Let's get out of here.'

Harry Leroy was standing, frozen, in front of the reinforced glass door, watching as the police car pulled slowly into the forecourt. And, loud now, the sound of police sirens, close and getting closer.

'Out!' Rawlings shouted. 'Out, out, now.'

Josh and Casper hurled themselves at the back door, locked with a bar across, and only succeeded in setting off an alarm.

'Move!' Rawlings yelled at Leroy and when he didn't budge, clubbed him with the barrel of the gun.

By then a second car had come skidding across the forecourt, narrowly avoiding collision with the petrol pumps, officers jumping out wearing protective vests, weapons drawn.

Rawlings leaped back towards the counter and grabbed Dawn by the arm, gun pointed at her face, and she swung the fire extinguisher she'd been holding behind her back. and struck him on the shoulder, hard enough to knock the gun aside. Swung again and caught him on the side of the head as he backed away.

Rawlings staggered, almost but not quite falling to his knees.

A police officer stood in the open doorway, a semi-automatic machine gun pointing at Rawlings' chest. He could feel blood running down onto his neck. His fingers opened and the air pistol slid to the floor. Tears flooded his eyes.

A second officer, armed with a 9mm handgun, ordered him to lay, face down, on the floor.

Jackie Ferris crossed to where Dawn was still standing, shaking, close to hyperventilating, and slowly prised the fire extinguisher from her hand.

'What was that all about before?' Nick asked, as Marcus passed through the kitchen. 'Sirens and everything.'

'Something going on at the petrol station, apparently. Some kind of robbery.'

Nick pulled off his apron, heading for the door.

By the time he arrived, breathless, chest aching, his mum and Jackie Ferris were sitting outside on the low wall, sharing a cigarette. The first drags Ferris had allowed herself in almost two years. Rawlings and company had already been carted away.

'What happened?' Nick asked.

'It doesn't matter,' Dawn said, getting to her feet. 'Not now.'

'Are you all right?'

'Yes, I'm fine.'

'Then tell me.'

Behind them, Jackie Ferris stubbed out the cigarette and walked away.

Dawn held out her arms and hugged Nick close enough for him to feel her shake. 'I'll tell you later, okay?'

CHAPTER 27

It was two or three nights later that Nick walked up onto the bridge. The clock by his bed had read 02:42 and he'd been awake for hours, unable to get back to sleep. A voice he thought he recognised sounding in his head.

From where he stood now, he could look down through the railings to the road below, few cars at that time, the occasional lorry, little more. The sky was clear and filled with stars and for a moment Nick thought it was like looking up at the ceiling in his room. Only more so. The moon was almost full.

In the distance, never quite dark, the centre of the city rose against a faint orange glow.

Nick shivered and pulled his leather jacket close.

'Not about to do anything silly, are you?'

Nick turned at his father's voice and, expecting nothing, saw his father walking slowly towards him, still wearing the clothes in which he'd seen him last, blue cotton workman's jacket, basketball boots, blue jeans.

'No,' Nick said, a slight tingling at the back of the neck.

'One in the family enough, eh?'

'Something like that.'

'So?' his father said. 'Surprised to see me?'

'Yes, I suppose so.' And yet he wasn't, not really.

'You think I've got some apologising to do.'

'Bit late for that.'

'Yes, well . . . I've always wanted to, you know. Apologise to you and your mum. For what I did. Only . . .' He smiled. 'I could never figure out what to say.'

'The truth?'

'What's that?'

'Why you did it.'

'Why I jumped?'

'What else?'

'Oh, God, Nick, half a hundred things.'

'This was the one that mattered.'

His father was standing close to him now, close enough for Nick to feel his breath, ice cold, on his face.

For some little while he didn't speak.

Neither of them spoke.

'There was this look,' his father finally said, 'would come into your mum's eyes. Something I'd not done, some little thing. Not so little sometimes, I suppose. And she'd get this look, this way of telling me, showing how she was disappointed. Not surprised. And you – Christ, Nick, you know sometimes I'd go into your room when you were asleep and look at you lying there, arms spread wide, eyes closed, and know that sooner or later that same look of disappointment would be on your face as well. Each time you saw me. Whenever I walked into the room. And I couldn't wait for that to happen.'

'Maybe it wouldn't have. Maybe it would've been different.'

His father looked away.

'Do you ever think of that?' Nick said, suddenly angry. 'Do you?'

'Only every day.'

Nick closed his eyes.

'All my life, Nick,' his father said, 'I said no to things, all kinds of things, stayed in my own little world, found excuses for turning them down.'

'You stuck to what you believed in,' Nick said.

'Look where that got me,' his father said and laughed.

Nick wanted to hug him, hold his hand.

'Your mum, she's okay?'

'Yes, I think so.'

'That business where she works . . .'

'You know about that?'

'She was brave.'

'Yes, she was.'

'And you? How's school?'

Nick shrugged. 'You know.'

'You've taken up the guitar.'

'I don't know for how long.'

'Maybe it's not your thing.'

'Maybe.'

'Photography, though . . .'

Nick smiled.

'And the girl? Ellen, is it?'

'What about her?'

'Stop thinking you're not good enough for her, that's all.'

'Is that what I'm thinking?'

And suddenly he was no longer there. Nick leaned back against the bridge and felt the iron of the railings hard against his back and arms. The stars, some of them, had been swallowed up by clouds. So many more questions he had wanted to ask. Maybe if he waited, patient, believed, there would be another chance.

Starting to walk, he felt a little sick, a little hollow inside.

But not for long.

Tomorrow, he thought, as he walked down the steps, I'll give Ellen a call, see what she's doing at the weekend. Get her to come somewhere with me. Take the camera, maybe.

He quickened his pace as he realised tomorrow was only a few hours away.

ACKNOWLEDGEMENTS

My thanks are due to Nat Boon, Joshua Held and Rebecca Ratty for reading earlier versions of the manuscript and making positive and useful suggestions; thanks also to Tom Harvey and Liz Simcock for musical advice and, especially, to Hylda Sims for sharing her memories of the early British blues and folk scene and her skiffling days – and nights – with The City Ramblers. Above all, thank you to my French publisher, François Guerif, for the initial suggestion.